SNAP, CRACKLE, GULP

Everyone was in a mood to match the swamp. After a hasty breakfast, they packed up and moved to the boats.

The same trooper who had been last on sentry duty stepped to the rope that secured one and stooped to unfasten it.

The water exploded. Out of it hurtled a reptilian behemoth, its jaws spread wide. Before the trooper could recoil or cry out, the alligator's mouth clamped shut with awful force. Bones cracked and blood spurted, and the next instant the gator was hauling its quarry back into the water.

It happened so fast, everyone was rooted in shock.

Fargo recovered first, and snapping the Henry to his shoulder, he took a hasty bead between the alligator's eyes. He thumbed back the hammer—and the gator went under. . . .

THE
TRAILSMAN
#375

TEXAS
SWAMP FEVER

by

Jon Sharpe

A SIGNET BOOK

SIGNET
Published by New American Library, a division of
Penguin Group (USA) Inc., 375 Hudson Street,
New York, New York 10014, USA
Penguin Group (Canada), 90 Eglinton Avenue East, Suite 700, Toronto,
Ontario M4P 2Y3, Canada (a division of Pearson Penguin Canada Inc.)
Penguin Books Ltd., 80 Strand, London WC2R 0RL, England
Penguin Ireland, 25 St. Stephen's Green, Dublin 2,
Ireland (a division of Penguin Books Ltd.)
Penguin Group (Australia), 250 Camberwell Road, Camberwell, Victoria 3124,
Australia (a division of Pearson Australia Group Pty. Ltd.)
Penguin Books India Pvt. Ltd., 11 Community Centre, Panchsheel Park,
New Delhi - 110 017, India
Penguin Group (NZ), 67 Apollo Drive, Rosedale, Auckland 0632,
New Zealand (a division of Pearson New Zealand Ltd.)
Penguin Books (South Africa) (Pty.) Ltd., 24 Sturdee Avenue,
Rosebank, Johannesburg 2196, South Africa

Penguin Books Ltd., Registered Offices:
80 Strand, London WC2R 0RL, England

First published by Signet, an imprint of New American Library,
a division of Penguin Group (USA) Inc.

First Printing, January 2013
10 9 8 7 6 5 4 3 2 1

The first chapter of this book previously appeared in *Fort Death*, the three
hundred seventy-fourth volume in this series.

 REGISTERED TRADEMARK—MARCA REGISTRADA

Printed in the United States of America

PUBLISHER'S NOTE
This is a work of fiction. Names, characters, places, and incidents either are the
product of the author's imagination or are used fictitiously, and any resemblance to
actual persons, living or dead, business establishments, events, or locales is entirely
coincidental.

The publisher does not have any control over and does not assume any responsi-
bility for author or third-party Web sites or their content.

The Trailsman

Beginnings . . . they bend the tree and they mark the man. Skye Fargo was born when he was eighteen. Terror was his midwife, vengeance his first cry. Killing spawned Skye Fargo, ruthless, cold-blooded murder. Out of the acrid smoke of gunpowder still hanging in the air, he rose, cried out a promise never forgotten.

The Trailsman they began to call him all across the West: searcher, scout, hunter, the man who could see where others only looked, his skills for hire but not his soul, the man who lived each day to the fullest, yet trailed each tomorrow. Skye Fargo, the Trailsman, the seeker who could take the wildness of a land and the wanting of a woman and make them his own.

1861, the Texas swamp country—
where there are a hundred ways to die.

1

If looks could kill, Skye Fargo would be dead. He saw distrust and dislike on every face, in every glare.

A big man, wide at the shoulders and slim at the waist, he rode into Suttree's Landing with his right hand on his hip above his Colt. His lake blue eyes betrayed no more concern than if he was out for a stroll in a Saint Louis park, but Suttree's Landing was a far cry from a civilized city like Saint Louis. It was a backwater hamlet at the edge of the Archaletta Swamp, and the people were suspicious of strangers.

Fargo didn't care. He had a job to do, and any jackass who gave him trouble would find out the hard way he wasn't a cheek-turner.

The Landing wasn't anything to brag about. Most of the people lived in shabby shacks that wouldn't stand up to a strong prairie wind. But there wasn't much wind in the swamp, except when it stormed.

The general store, the hub of commerce for miles around, alone among all the buildings in the hamlet had glass in its windows.

The people were a mix of white and half bloods and a few Indians. Tame Indians, they were called, to set them apart from the wild ones that lived deep in the shadowed haunts of the vast swamp.

Sullen, sharp-eyed, the inhabitants watched Fargo and those behind him come down what passed for a street. On every face was the stamp of hardship and poverty, even the children.

Fargo drew rein at a hitch rail and dismounted.

Several locals were lounging against the wall and eyed him much as hungry wolves might eye a buck. Unshaven and unkempt, they wore clothes that a Saint Louis beggar wouldn't be caught dead in.

One had a wad in his cheek and spat brown juice near the Ovaro's front hoof, which brought snickers from the others.

Fargo stared at him until the spitter shifted his weight and frowned.

"I don't much like being looked at, mister."

"Spit at my horse again and you won't have a mouth to spit with."

The man smirked. "Is that right?"

Fargo placed his hand on his Colt. "It sure as hell is."

Some of the smug went out of the spitter. "You'd shoot a man who ain't heeled?" All he had around his waist was a middling-sized knife.

"A man spits on my horse," Fargo said, "he has it coming."

"Here now," said a beanpole in a shirt two sizes too small. "You can't just ride in and talk about shootin' folks."

"That's right," spoke up a heavyset brute with more eyebrow than forehead. "Bodean can spit where he damn well pleases."

Their tone made Fargo bristle. "Anytime any of you reckon you are man enough," he said.

The beanpole straightened and his thin lips curled back from yellow teeth. "Listen to you. You think you're the cock of the walk, don't you?"

"It's easy enough to find out."

By then the rest of Fargo's party had filed out of the woods and drawn rein. The lead rider, who sat ramrod straight in his saddle and didn't seem entirely comfortable in his store-bought suit, cleared his throat.

"That will be quite enough, if you please, Mr. Fargo. I'm sure these gentlemen meant no disrespect."

"Like hell they didn't," Fargo said.

2

The lead rider climbed down. Only a few inches over five feet, he carried himself as if he were taller. His boots were polished to a shine and the revolver on his left hip was worn in a holster with a flap. He nodded at the swamp rats and said, "How do you do. I'm Ma—" Catching himself, he changed it to, "I'm James Davenport. Would this be Franklyn Suttree's establishment?"

"Franklyn?" the spitter said, and snorted. "Hereabouts we call him Sutty."

"Ain't you somethin'?" the beanpole said, "in your fancy duds."

"City boy," said the one with eyebrows like thick caterpillars.

Davenport wheeled on him. "I'm older than you, I'll have you know."

Fargo couldn't resist. "Take it easy," he said, and threw Davenport's remark back at him. "I'm sure these gentlemen meant no disrespect."

Just then another member of their party dismounted. Even taller than Fargo, he had arms as thick as tree trunks and a face that might have been forged on an anvil. He, too, wore a new store-bought suit. He, too, wore a flapped holster. "Is there a problem, sir?" he asked Davenport. "Say the word and we'll deal with it."

"That won't be necessary, Mr. Morgan," Davenport said.

The rest of their party were climbing down.

Fargo saw the three locals give a start and their mouths fall open, and he knew why without turning. The next moment he smelled her perfume, and inwardly swore. He'd been against bringing her but the government insisted she had to come.

"We've finally arrived," Clementine Purdy declared. "I swear, it took us forever to get here." She had big green eyes and full red lips and a bosom that bulged farther than most. A bonnet contained brunette curls and her shoes were of the finest calf leather.

"Hell, lady," Fargo responded in annoyance, "we haven't even started yet."

Davenport frowned. "Need I remind you that she *is* a lady, and an important one? I'll thank you to watch your language around her."

"Please," Clementine Purdy said. "Mr. Fargo may speak as he pleases."

"Not while I'm in charge," Davenport said.

Fargo noticed that Bodean and the other two were listening with keen interest.

"In charge of what, mister?" Bodean asked. "Who are you folks, anyhow?"

"We're a hunting party out of Galveston," Davenport fed them the lie.

Fargo had warned the major that few if any of the locals would believe it, and he could see by the expressions on Bodean and his two friends that he had been right.

"You came all this way to hunt?" the beanpole said skeptically. "Ain't there any deer and bear around about Galveston?"

Davenport adopted a knowing smile. "If deer and bear were all we were after, we could have spared ourselves the trip. But we're after more dangerous game. A type that abounds in this great swamp of yours." He paused. "We're after alligators."

The beetling brows of the heavyset man met over his nose. "There's plenty of gators hereabouts, sure enough. But I never heard tell of folks comin' all the way from Galveston or anywhere else to hunt 'em."

"Damned peculiar," Bodean said.

"There's a first time for everything," Davenport cheerfully told them.

"Why in hell would you want to hunt gators?" the beanpole asked.

"I've hunted for years," Davenport expanded on his lie. "Everything under the sun, from grizzly and mountain sheep in the Rockies to buffalo and antelope on the prairie. Now I intend to try my hand at something new. Game that will challenge my mettle."

"Challenge your what?"

"Test my ability," Davenport said.

"Gators?" Bodean said.

"Gators," Davenport said, and motioned at Fargo and Morgan and Clementine Purdy and the four other men in new store-bought suits. "We'll be heading into the swamp in the morning and will require the services of a guide. Perhaps you would be so kind as to spread the word?"

"Mister," the beanpole said. "My name is Cleon, and I've lived in this swamp all my life. Take my advice and turn around and go home. It ain't no place for you and yours."

"It's where the gators are," Davenport said.

"And a lot more things, besides," Cleon said. "There's water moccasins and copperheads. There's bogs and quicksand. There's swamp bears, which are meaner than any you'll find in your Rockies, and painters, cats that can pull a man from his horse and drag him off—"

"You exaggerate, surely," Davenport said.

". . . and there's the Injuns," Cleon went on as if he hadn't heard. "Some are peaceable but a lot more ain't. You could end up in their cookin' pot if'n you ain't careful."

"Are you suggesting some of them are cannibals?" Davenport said.

"Used to be a lot that were, back in the old days. Now it's just the one tribe but that one tribe is enough." Cleon lowered his voice almost to a whisper. "Ain't you heard of the Kilatku?"

The Kilatku were just one of scores of little-known tribes that lived in the uncharted watery fastness along the Texas and Louisiana coasts. Where a lot of the other tribes had at least some dealings with whites, the Kilatku had none whatsoever. Every white man who dared enter their territory never came out again. It was part of the reason Fargo and the others were there, and about to risk their lives in what he considered a damn silly enterprise.

"You talk too much," Bodean snapped at Cleon.

"They've got a female, consarn you," Cleon said. "They need to know."

"We look after our own, not outsiders," Bodean growled. He unfurled and headed up the street. "We've talked to them enough. Let's go." He pointed at the man with the caterpillar eyebrows. "You, too, Judson."

"Charming fellow," Davenport said.

"A viper is more like it," Fargo said.

Clementine Purdy adjusted her bonnet. "Really, Mr. Fargo. I've only known you a short while but you strike me as terribly cynical. The gentleman called Cleon warned us about the Kilatku, didn't he?"

"You already knew about them."

"We were all thoroughly briefed," Clementine said. "We know what we are letting ourselves in for."

"No, you don't."

"I beg your pardon?"

"You have no damn idea what you're in for, but you're going into the swamp anyway."

"So are you and Major Davenport and Sergeant Morgan and these other soldiers," Clementine said.

"We're men," Fargo said.

"Ah." Clementine scowled. "And you consider me a frail female. Is that it?" She sniffed and said, "We all have our duty to perform, I'll have you know."

"Just so it doesn't get us killed," Fargo said.

2

The general store wasn't cozy and clean, like most. It was dusty and dark and there was an odor Fargo couldn't quite peg that made him want to cover his nose.

Merchandise was heaped on shelves and in bins and barrels in no particular order. Knives, tools, boots, traps of different sizes, whale oil for lamps, lucifers; it had everything a person would need to live and survive in the great swamp.

None of it was particularly well kept. Many of the knives and tools had spots of rust. Most of the clothes were used. Instead of a cracker barrel or a pickle barrel there was a salt barrel. Hides hung from the walls, some of them moth-eaten.

Clementine Purdy scrunched up her nose and said, "My word."

Davenport strode to the counter, his hands behind his back, looking as natural and relaxed as a cat in a room full of rocking chairs. "How do you do, my good man," he addressed the proprietor. "I take it you are Franklyn Suttree?"

The big-bellied owner wore clothes that hadn't seen water in a month of Sundays. He was greasy and dirty and a fly was crawling on his hair. He'd been leaning on his elbows and chewing a toothpick and watching them as if he couldn't quite believe what he was seeing. "How do, yourself," he said. "Folks call me Sutty."

"We have it on reliable authority that you are the man to

see about conveyance into the interior of the Archaletta," Davenport said.

"Huh?" Sutty straightened. "Can you say that again in little words?"

Fargo noticed a dead rat hanging by twine from a rafter. "We hear you rent boats."

"Oh," Sutty said. "Who told you that?"

"Friends of ours," Davenport said.

"Who might they be?"

"That's hardly relevant," Davenport said. "We'd like to rent four of your best."

"Would you, now?" Sutty said, and snickered. "I only got two and one has a slow leak."

"Only two?" Davenport said. "But there are eight of us, plus all our supplies and gear." He gazed about him as if expecting to see the boats in the store. "How big are these boats of yours?"

"How about I show you," Sutty said. He lumbered around the counter and over to a narrow hall. "Follow me, folks."

The smells in the back were even worse. Fargo saw a partially butchered hog in one room and in another a gray-haired woman sat in a rocking chair, knitting and chewing tobacco.

The back door opened onto the landing. Over half a dozen boats of different kinds were tied up, along with several canoes.

Sutty walked over to a pair of boats that appeared to have been built about the time of the Great Flood. Both had flat bottoms and square prows and were about ten feet long and four feet wide. "Here's my two," he announced. "They might not look like much but they'll get you in and out again."

"They aren't enough," Davenport said.

"They're all I got."

Davenport motioned. "What about these others? Some of them are in a lot better condition."

"Don't your ears work? They're not mine."

"I mean," Davenport said, "do you think their owners would let us use them in return for fair compensation?"

"There you go again," Sutty said. "Can't you talk plain like everybody else?"

"Just answer his question," Morgan said.

"Now, now," Davenport said. "I'll thank you to permit me to handle this."

"I don't like how these bumpkins treat us, sir," Morgan said.

"And I don't like bein' called no bumpkin," Sutty said. "Find your damn boats somewhere else."

Fargo decided to intervene. "We're renting yours," he said.

"Not if I don't let you, you ain't," Sutty said.

Hooking his thumb in his gun belt close to his holster, Fargo locked eyes. "You're letting us."

Sutty opened his mouth, glanced at the Colt and at Fargo's face, and closed it again. He coughed and said, "You're not like these others."

"No," Fargo said. "I'm not."

"I don't like them much."

Fargo shrugged. "They are who they are."

Sutty slowly nodded as if he understood. "How'd you get stuck with them?"

"I'm doing a friend a favor."

Sutty did more nodding. "Favors will bite you on the ass every time."

"What are you two talking about?" Davenport broke in. "Let's stay focused on the boats." He regarded a flatbed, the newest of them all. "Mr. Suttree, would you send word to the owners of these craft and inquire whether they might be willing to rent them to us? Especially this one. Inform them that I'm willing to pay any fee they want, within reason, of course."

"I can do that, yes, if'n you pay me five dollars," Sutty

said. "And they'll want to know for how long, and how far in you aim to go."

"As I explained to Bodean and his companions," Davenport said, "we're after alligators. I plan to have the biggest I can shoot stuffed and mounted to add to my trophies."

"Just when I think I've heard it all."

"We'll also need a guide," Davenport mentioned. "Someone dependable. We're willing to pay top dollar for their services."

"Are you, now?" Sutty said, and wiped his sweaty hands on his dirty apron. "It could be a day or two before you hear about the other boats and the guide."

"I was hoping to leave in the morning," Davenport said.

"You want me to spread word or not?"

"Yes, by all means." Davenport gazed at the hamlet. "Is there somewhere we can put up for the night? A boarding-house, perhaps, since I see no evidence of a hotel."

"God in heaven, mister," Sutty said. "Where do you think you are?"

"What?" Davenport said.

"There's the woods," Sutty said, and pointed. "Camp wherever you want."

Clementine said, "We've done so much of that already. What I wouldn't give for a nice, soft bed."

Fargo smothered a grin. He wouldn't mind getting her into a nice, soft bed himself.

"I got to find some boys to spread your word," Sutty said, and made for his store.

Staring after him, Davenport said, "This isn't proceeding exactly as planned."

"Say the word, Major," Morgan said, "and we'll commandeer as many boats as you need."

"And arouse their anger?" Davenport shook his head. "I think not. Besides, they'd demand to know by what authority we presume to take their boats, and learn who we are."

"Not if we don't tell them, sir," Morgan said.

"We can't be high-handed about this, Sergeant," Davenport said. "We're under orders, remember?"

"Yes, sir."

"And stop calling me sir so long as we're at the Landing," Davenport directed. "Someone might overhear and suspect."

"Yes, s—" Morgan caught himself. "Yes, Mr. Davenport, whatever you say."

Davenport turned to Fargo. "It's promising, don't you think?"

"We haven't dipped a paddle yet," Fargo said.

"Even so, a day or two delay is worth it if we acquire at least one more boat and a guide."

"What will you tell him?" Fargo asked.

"Suttree? About what?"

"The guide. You can't come right out and say you want to go into Kilatku territory. No one in their right mind will take you."

"Surely there's a soul brave enough to dare the danger."

"You're thinking like a military man," Fargo said. "These people fight shy of the Kilatkus. They want nothing to do with them."

"We'll pay him extra," Davenport said. "That should suffice."

Fargo motioned at the run-down buildings and the people in their hand-me-downs. "Do they look like they care that much about money?"

"Everyone likes money," Davenport said. "These poor wretches most of all."

Fargo reminded himself to be patient. The major was from New England and had grown up in a well-to-do family.

"Frankly," Davenport said, "I'm surprised you can't guide us."

"I've never been here before," Fargo said.

"Which has me wondering why General Powell insisted I bring you along."

"He's a friend," Fargo said. "I've scouted for him a few

times." He'd also saved the general's life once, but he didn't bring that up. "I'm doing this as a favor."

"Doing what, exactly?" Davenport asked. "You can't guide us. You're not a trooper. You're not with the Office of Indian Affairs; Miss Purdy is. What purpose do you serve?"

Fargo was honest with him. "The general wants me to help keep you and your people alive."

"How, when you just admitted you've never been to the Archaletta Swamp? What can you do that we can't?" Davenport's brows knit in puzzlement. "It makes no sense. But then, I follow orders, whether they do or they don't." He went over to Morgan and said something and the pair walked toward the street.

Fargo sighed. It wasn't something Major Davenport would understand. General Powell did, only because the general had fought the Sioux and the Comanches and lived in Apache country for a year and a half.

"I know I'm asking a lot," Powell had told him the night before they left Fort Leavenworth. "Major Davenport is highly competent, and I personally picked Sergeant Morgan and those under him. They're all good soldiers, but that isn't enough. They don't have that instinct you do, the instinct to survive, no matter what it takes. I'm counting on you to keep them alive." He'd paused. "I'm counting on you to keep *her* alive."

Fargo had promised to do his best. He'd been to the bayou country a few times, so it wasn't as if he was green when it came to swamps and their perils. But there was only so much he could do.

It didn't help that shapely and luscious Clementine Purdy was a powerful distraction. All the way to Texas, he couldn't stop imagining her naked, squirming under him as he ran his hands over every square inch of her—

"A penny for your thoughts?" asked the vision of loveliness herself.

Fargo turned, and smiled. He might as well test the waters. "I was wondering whether you moan when you make love."

To his surprise, Clementine didn't bat an eye. "I wouldn't know," she said sweetly.

"Why not?" Fargo asked.

"I never have."

3

The rest of the afternoon, Fargo couldn't get it out of his head. He thought about it as they climbed on their horses and rode into the woods to a clearing. He thought about it as he helped chop wood for the fire and as he waited for trooper Weaver to brew coffee. He thought about it as he sat sipping from his tin cup and envisioning her without her clothes on.

The shadows were lengthening with the setting of the sun when Fargo roused and walked over to where Major Davenport and Clementine were seated on a log, talking and having a grand time.

"Mr. Fargo," Davenport said. "What can we do for you?"

"I'll be at Suttree's Landing until midnight or so," Fargo informed him. "Reckoned you should know."

"How considerate," Davenport said. "But in case you've forgotten, I'm in charge. No one goes anywhere without my permission."

"In case you've forgotten," Fargo rejoined, "I'm not working for the army. I'm doing this because General Powell asked me to."

"Are you suggesting that you're free to do as you please?" Davenport made it sound as if the idea were preposterous. "If so, you're wrong. You were assigned to my command and I expect you to follow orders like everyone else."

"Midnight," Fargo said, and turned to go.

"Don't force me to have Sergeant Morgan restrain you," the officer warned.

"He's welcome to try."

Davenport stiffened and raised an arm toward where Morgan and the four troopers were seated. "I'll call him over and then we'll see."

"Gentlemen, please," Clementine spoke up. "I'm sure my uncle wouldn't like for you to squabble like this."

Major Davenport didn't hide his surprise. "Your uncle?"

Clementine Purdy nodded. "General Powell. My mother's older brother. Her maiden name is Powell. The only reason Mr. Fargo is here is because she asked Uncle Thomas to keep an eye on me and he sent for the best man for the job."

"And he picked me," Fargo said in amusement. The general was well aware of his fondness for the ladies.

"Uncle Tom told me that if anyone can bring me back alive, it's you," Clementine said.

"I'll be damned."

"Even so," Davenport said, "I won't have you going off to get drunk."

"Major," Fargo said, "it could be someone knows something about the surveyor and his people."

"What more is there to learn?" Davenport said. "The man was commissioned to make the first-ever survey of the Archaletta Swamp. He was at it several months when he went into Kilatku territory and never returned. Now we've been asked to escort and protect Miss Purdy in her efforts to establish peaceful relations with them so a new surveyor can be brought in and the survey completed."

"Maybe the Kilatku don't want peace," Fargo felt compelled to note.

"Nonsense," Clementine said. "I'll convince them it's in their own best interests. When they see the trade goods I've brought, they'll want more."

"A few blankets and mirrors and knives won't stop them from slitting our throats," Fargo predicted.

"It's more than a few," Clementine said, "and how do you

know it won't? Most tribes are eager to trade with whites. It's how we civilize them."

"Personally, I prefer a saber," Davenport said. "But whatever works to keep the heathens in line."

So the major was one of *those,* Fargo reflected.

"Midnight," he said again, and got out of there before he said something that would make the major mad.

Heathens, hell. Fargo had lived with Indians. Ate and drank with them and slept in their lodges. To his way of thinking, they were fine as they were. They didn't need civilizing. He didn't condone the killing the hostile tribes did, but he'd do the same if it was his land the whites were invading.

His saddle creaked under him as he swung on and gigged the Ovaro. He was sincere about trying to learn more about the surveyor. He also wanted a drink.

Across the street from Sutty's stood a building with batwings. It had no sign, and didn't need one. The batwings were enough.

As Fargo drew rein, he could smell the liquor.

Lamps were being lit, and many a window cast a rosy glow in the gathering dark. Few people were abroad. It was the supper hour.

Fargo pushed on the batwings and strode in. He was expecting a typical saloon but nothing about Suttree's Landing was typical.

The floor was dirt, the bar a long plank set on overturned barrels. The tables were squares of pine, the chairs too small. Several locals were playing poker, and the barman was helping himself to a glass of rum.

"Monongahela, if you have it," Fargo said.

"You must be the buckskin with those city folks everyone is gabbin' about." The man offered his hand. "They call me Cotton on account of I'm from Georgia."

"What else are people saying?" Fargo wondered.

"That you're a pack of liars, and government liars, at

that. Expectin' us to believe you came all this way to shoot gators."

"Why government?" Fargo asked.

"Folks have seen how those others parade around," Cotton said. "That Davenport, and the big one. They act like they have a broom shoved up their ass. And who else does that but the government?"

"What's your best guess?"

"Some think you're lawmen but none of you wear badges. And then there's the female. She has everyone stumped. She's pretty and sweet and doesn't put on airs like that Davenport fella."

"How about me?"

"You ain't no city boy," Cotton said. "Sutty says you don't take guff, and you've got mean eyes when you're riled." He looked Fargo up and down. "My guess about you? Damn me if I don't take you for a scout."

"I've done my share," Fargo admitted.

"I knew it," Cotton crowed. "It's how you carry yourself. You're a wolf, and you can bite. One look and anyone with sense would leave you be."

"You'd be surprised," Fargo said, "at how many don't have any."

Cotton placed a bottle and a glass in front of him. "Help yourself."

"Obliged." Fargo smiled as the drink spread a familiar warmth. He poured a second with his mouth still wet from the first.

"You like your liquor," Cotton observed.

"Almost as much as I like doves." Fargo gazed about the nearly empty saloon. "It's a shame you don't have any."

"Stick around. It's early yet. You're in for a surprise."

Since the man was being so friendly, Fargo ventured to say, "There was another outfit came through here about this time a year ago. Do you remember them?"

"Sure do," Cotton said. "That surveyor, Williams, and his helpers. They were workin' on a survey for the government." He snorted. "Jackasses. Sayin' as how they were goin' to survey the whole blamed swamp."

"Did you talk to them?"

"Sure did," Cotton said. "Williams was a drinker. Scotch, as I recollect. He'd come in here every night he was at the Landin'. Got to know him pretty well. Nice fella, but dumb."

"Oh?"

"They'd go off into the swamp for a couple of weeks and come back and rest up and he'd send a report off, and then they'd go off again and do more surveyin'. It went on like that for a good long while."

"And then one time they went off and never came back," Fargo said.

Cotton nodded.

"Any idea what happened?"

"They went into Kilatku country. That was the last anyone saw of them."

"You're sure that's where they went?" Fargo would hate to think he was about to risk his hide over a mistake.

"Williams himself stood about where you're standin' right now and told me what he was about to do. I tried to talk him out of it. I said the Kilatku would stuff him in a pot and eat him. But would he listen?" Cotton shook his head. "He said he'd brought trinkets to give them so they'd let him survey. Knowin' them, they threw his damn trinkets in the swamp and ate him down to the bone."

"You know for a fact they're cannibals?"

"I ain't ever seen them eat anybody," Cotton said. "But the tame Indians say they do, and I'm not one of those who disbelieves an Injun just because his skin happens to be red and mine ain't."

"Me either."

"A survey, of all things," Cotton said in amazement. "Why the hell does the government need to survey a *swamp*?

Everyone knows what's out there. Water and gators and snakes." His eyes narrowed. "Is your outfit connected to theirs somehow?"

Before Fargo could answer, the batwings squeaked wide and in strode Bodean, Cleon and Judson. Bodean stopped short and said something out of the corner of his mouth to Judson and the pair advanced on the bar.

"Uh-oh," Cotton said so only Fargo heard. "Better watch yourself. Those two are trouble."

"So am I," Fargo said, and calmly poured a third drink.

"Lookee here," Bodean said, coming up on his right and leaning on an elbow. "If it isn't High-and-Mighty his own self."

Judson came up on the left so they had him boxed.

Cleon, though, hung back. He clearly didn't want any part of it.

"Where's your friends?" Bodean asked.

"Not here," Fargo said.

"I didn't ask you where they're not, I asked you where they are." Bodean glanced at the shelf of bottles and grinned. "Tell you what. How about you buy us drinks?"

"How about I don't," Fargo said, and sipped and set down his glass. It would take them a minute to work up to it.

Bodean looked at Judson. "Not very neighborly of him, is it?"

"Sure ain't," Judson said.

"I don't like you, mister," Bodean said, and poked Fargo in the ribs. "Not even a little bit. Give us an excuse and we'll pound you into the dirt."

"You need an excuse?" Fargo said, and punched him in the face.

4

Caught unprepared, Bodean rocked onto his heels. He tottered and grabbed at the bar to keep from falling.

Fargo started to turn but Judson was quicker than he looked, and brawny arms wrapped around him from behind, pinning his own.

"I got him!"

Bodean recovered his balance. He touched his hand to blood trickling from his bottom lip, and swore. "Hold him, Jud. I'm about to hurt him real bad." He balled his fists and took a step but stopped and glared at Cleon. "Why are you just standin' there? Help us pound on him."

Cleon shook his head. "I don't want no part of this."

"Why in hell not? He just hit me."

"You were proddin'," Cleon said.

Bodean shook a fist. "When I'm done with him, I'm goin' to whale the tar out of you."

"Damn it, Bodean," Cleon said. "You're always causin' trouble."

Their spat gave Fargo time to set himself. Now, with a powerful surge, he slammed his head back even as he exerted all his strength against the arms pinning him.

Judson grunted, and wet drops spattered the nape of Fargo's neck. Then he was free, and moved away from the bar.

Judson had a hand to his nose, which poured scarlet.

"We go at him together," Bodean said. "Two on one, we'll wear him down."

Judson bobbed his chin.

Fargo didn't feel particularly threatened. The pair were bumpkins. All bluster and no brains. He doubted that they had been in half as many fights as he had, and skill trumped stupid every time. "You get this one chance to turn and go."

"Scared, are you?" Bodean smirked. "You've stepped in it and now your yellow streak is showin'."

"I just don't want to scuff my knuckles on your teeth."

"Listen to him," Judson growled. "Let's do this!"

They came in sure but slow, their arms cocked, leading with their left legs and their left fists.

Inwardly, Fargo smiled. They had no idea what they were in for.

Bodean launched a right cross that Fargo blocked and then drove a right of his own that split Bodean's cheek. Judson sought to take advantage by flicking a jab at Fargo's unprotected side but Fargo lowered his elbow to absorb the brunt and swung a looping right that caught Judson on the side of the jaw and made his knees wobble.

Bodean lunged, trying to grab Fargo's arm, and Fargo clipped him on the ear.

Both swamp rats backed off, Judson shaking his head to clear it.

"Boys!" Cotton hollered. "That's enough. I don't want my place busted up."

"Butt out or we'll bust you," Bodean warned.

"You should listen to Cotton," Cleon coaxed. "No one has been hurt yet."

"I think my nose is broke," Judson said.

"And what do you call this?" Bodean said, jabbing a finger at his split cheek.

"We're not quittin'," Judson declared. "No one busts my nose unless I bust his back."

"Damn it all," Cleon said.

Fargo didn't say a thing. He waited, fists up.

He didn't have to wait long.

"We don't stop until he's down," Bodean said, and waded in, swinging wildly.

Fargo ducked, backpedaled, sidestepped.

Judson hung back, apparently waiting for an opening.

With a fierce yell, Bodean drove an uppercut at Fargo's chin. Fargo countered with a forearm and delivered an uppercut of his own. He thought he heard teeth crunch. A fist slammed his body, and he winced. Judson was on him, arms pumping. He warded off more blows but his collarbone and then his side spiked with pain. He rammed a straight-arm that sent Judson staggering.

"Damn you," Bodean raged, spitting out bits of broken tooth.

"Our fists ain't workin'," Judson said. "It should be knives."

"Not in here!" Cotton shouted. "I won't have no killin'."

Judson reached for the knife on his hip but Cleon came out of nowhere and seized his wrist.

"No, consarn you. So far it's been harmless but a blade means buryin'."

"Harmless, hell," Bodean said, and spat more bloody bits. He dropped his hand to the hilt of his own knife.

Fargo decided to end it. A fistfight was one thing. A knife fight, one or more of them *would* need burying. Just like that, he had the Colt out and level. At the click of the hammer, Bodean and Judson froze.

"God Almighty," Cotton exclaimed. "Did you see him draw?"

Bodean jerked his hand off his knife. "Hold on there, mister. We don't have guns. It wouldn't be fair."

"Two on one is fair?" Fargo said.

"I'll cut you anyway," Judson growled, still striving to wrest free of Cleon.

"Let it be, boys," Cotton urged. "He licked you, and you should own up to it."

"Licked us, hell," Judson said.

Bodean rimmed his bloody lips with the tip of his tongue. "I reckon this has gone far enough, at that."

"What?" Judson said.

Holding both hands up, palms out, Bodean said, "I'm willin' to call a truce if you are, mister."

"This better be an end to it," Fargo told him.

"You don't know swamp folk if you think that," Judson said. With a sweep of his other arm, he cuffed Cleon, who fell back. Judson lunged, and suddenly found himself looking down the barrel of Fargo's Colt.

"Blink and I splatter your brains."

"Damn it, Judson," Bodean said. "Quit actin' the fool or you'll be dead."

Judson hissed like a kicked snake.

"Listen, mister," Bodean said, slowly sidling toward his friend. "How about if the two of us light a shuck? I give you my word he won't lift a finger against you."

Judson opened his mouth as if to disagree and Bodean grabbed his arm.

"Enough, goddamn you." Bodean pulled Judson toward the batwings. "He could kill you as easy as anything, you dumb son of a bitch."

Judson glowered at Fargo.

"See? We're leavin'," Bodean said. "No need for gunplay, is there?" At the batwings he shoved Judson ahead of him, and paused. "You and those others, mister. You shouldn't ought to have come. The swamp will bury you like it does all you outsiders." His mouth curled in a bloody grin. "And good riddance, I say."

The batwings swung shut and they were gone.

"They never did learn to leave well enough alone," Cleon said.

Fargo swung the Colt in his direction. "Where do you stand in this?"

"Hey now," Cleon said, backing up. "You saw me try to

stop them. They're my friends, but I'll be damned if I'll spill blood for them or have my own spilled because they're too pigheaded for their own good."

"Cleon isn't like them," Cotton said. "He's got more sense than they do."

Fargo twirled the Colt into his holster but kept his hand on it. "Are they backshooters?"

"No," Cleon replied, much too quickly.

"Why don't I believe you?"

"They won't *shoot* you. But I wouldn't put it past them to find some other way to get back at you. Steal your horse, maybe. Or put a hole in one of your boats. That sort of thing."

The mere thought of anyone stealing the Ovaro was enough to set Fargo's blood to boiling. "You better talk to your friends," he advised. "The next time I won't go so easy on them."

"I'm real sorry about this, mister," Cleon said, and he hurried on out.

"Well, now," Cotton said. "Wasn't that excitin'?"

"It helped pass the time." Fargo refilled his glass and stood so he could see the entrance and the front window. Outside, night had settled. "Didn't you say something about a dove?"

"Her name is Sadie," Cotton said. "She'll be here when she feels like it."

Fargo went on drinking. He was in no hurry to return to camp and have to put up with Major Davenport. The major was a seasoned soldier and highly competent but he was too damn bossy.

The batwings creaked and Fargo looked up, thinking it might be the woman called Sadie. Instead, Sergeant Morgan stood framed in the doorway. Morgan spied him and came over.

"Care for a drink?" Fargo offered, sliding the bottle toward him.

"I'm not here for that," Morgan informed him. "Have you seen Miss Purdy?"

"She isn't with the major?"

Morgan shook his head. "She disappeared on us about half an hour ago. Davenport has everyone out searching."

"Did she take her horse?"

"No. She mentioned earlier that she'd like to go for a walk."

"All by her lonesome?"

"She has a mind of her own, that one."

A body, too, Fargo thought. But he understood the major's concern. The woods weren't as dangerous as the swamp but they were no place for Purdy to be. There were bears. Snakes. Gators sometimes came out on land.

"Care to lend a hand?" Sergeant Morgan asked.

"I'll look around the Landing," Fargo said.

"Good. Then I'll go back and help the ma—" Morgan frowned. "Help Davenport." His civilian clothes couldn't hide his military bearing as he departed.

Fargo paid and took the bottle with him. He was halfway to the batwings when they parted yet again and in came a woman.

"Sadie!" Cotton greeted her. "Want me to set up the usual?"

"I sure do, sugar," the woman cheerfully replied, and saw Fargo. "Hello? What have we here?"

Fargo didn't know what he was expecting. A dove with a lot of miles on her, maybe. Or a swamp woman with no more appeal than a she-goat.

The female in front of him wasn't more than twenty. Her eyes were as blue as his, her dress new, her body an hourglass with thighs that went on forever. She flashed nice white teeth, placed her hands on her hips, and wriggled them invitingly. "See anything you like, big man?"

"Oh, hell," Fargo said.

5

Sadie sashayed up, crooked her finger, and hooked his chin. "You're awful easy on the eyes, handsome."

So much of her cleavage was visible, Fargo felt a twitch below his belt. "So are you," he said more huskily than he intended.

Sadie leaned closer. Her perfume was intoxicating. "I have a room," she whispered. "How about you and me pay it a visit?"

Fargo thought of Clementine Purdy. His lust fought with doing the right thing. Unfortunately, doing the right thing won. "Can I take you up on that in an hour or so?"

"You have somewhere you need to be?"

"I do," Fargo said. "Damn it."

Sadie laughed. "I won't let it hurt my feelin's, then. I can see in your eyes that you're interested."

Fargo stared at the junction of her legs. "You have no idea."

"An hour," Sadie said, stepping aside. "But not much longer, hear? I might get another offer and a workin' gal has to earn a livin'."

Fargo touched her cheek and went out before he changed his mind. He stopped to breathe deep of the muggy night air.

Suttree's Landing was dark save for lit windows here and there. The businesses were all closed, other than the liquor mill. A few people were out and about, men mostly. As was common with country folk, most were early to bed and early to rise.

Fargo prowled in search of Clementine Purdy. It wasn't far to the Landing so she might have done as he did. He went along the main street and up and down its short offshoots. He started at the swamp end and was almost to the end nearest the wood when he heard voices. A woman said something in anger, and a man laughed.

Fargo went around the next corner.

There Clementine was, awash in the faint glow from a cabin window, her back stiff, her arms folded, a portrait of indignation. She was tapping her foot and glaring at three men.

They had their backs to Fargo but he knew who they were.

"All we did was ask you to have a drink with us," Judson said.

"That ain't askin' too much," Bodean said. "And you owe us, after what your friend did."

"I don't know what you gentlemen are talking about," Clementine said. "And for the last time, I'll thank you to get out of my way and let me go about my business."

"What business would that be?" Judson asked.

Cleon had hung back and now said, "We shouldn't be doin' this. Those men she's with won't like it. That Fargo won't like it, and you've already tangled with him once."

"You're a damned nuisance," Bodean growled at him. "Why don't you go home and leave this to us."

Clementine said, "I'm warning you for the last time. Get out of my way."

"Why don't you try and make us?" Bodean taunted.

By then Fargo had come up unnoticed behind them. Hooking his thumb in his gun belt, he said casually, "How about if I try?"

Bodean and Judson spun, their hands sweeping to their knives. They both glanced at Fargo's Colt, and stopped cold.

Bodean's face was a mask of hate.

"Mr. Fargo," Clementine said. "These men were accosting me."

"I don't even know what that means," Judson said.

"All we did was talk to her," Bodean said. "We didn't lay a finger on the bitch."

"Yet," Fargo said, and motioned. "Run along or have your wicks snuffed. Your choice."

"Is that a threat?" Bodean said.

"Hell no," Fargo said, and smiled. "It's a promise."

Reluctantly, the pair backed away, Bodean saying, "We won't forget you for this or the other."

"Count on it," Judson said.

"You see me trembling?" Fargo said.

A sly look came over Bodean. "We know these parts," he said. "You don't."

"I know hot air when I hear it."

Wheeling, they melted into the night.

Fargo turned to Cleon.

"I told them to leave her be."

"That he did," Clementine confirmed.

"You need new friends," Fargo said.

Cleon started to follow them, and stopped. "We grew up together. They're not always so mean to me as they were just now."

"They'll get you killed one day."

"Maybe so, but I can't turn my back on them."

Cleon doffed his hat to the lady from the Office of Indian Affairs. "Sorry about how they behaved, ma'am. They ain't much for manners."

"They're despicable," Clementine said archly.

"Yes, ma'am." Cleon jammed his hat on, turned on a heel, and hastened away.

"I never," Clementine said after him. "Don't these bumpkins have any decency?"

"What are you doing here? The major has everyone out looking for you."

"Does he indeed?" Clementine said. "I can't go for a walk without you men thinking I need to be rescued? I'm not helpless."

"How about I take you back?"

"I don't need an escort. But I wouldn't mind the company."

Fargo fell into step, shortening his stride to match hers. "It's not entirely safe around here at night."

"Oh, please. I'm a grown woman. I can take care of myself."

"Not out here you can't."

"I won't be mollycoddled," Clementine said. "Just because I'm female, you men treat me as if I'm a helpless infant."

Fargo let his gaze rove her luscious figure. "Texas isn't Ohio." He recalled that was where she was from.

"What's that supposed to mean? Ohio is a perfectly fine state, I'll have you know."

"They wear guns in Ohio?"

"No. Of course not."

"Do you have hostiles in Ohio?"

"You know we don't."

"Buffalo? Grizzlies? Outlaws?"

"Oh. I see," Clementine said. "You're trying to impress on me how dangerous life is west of the Mississippi. Well, even so, I came prepared. I'm not defenseless."

"Prepared?" Fargo said.

From somewhere in her dress Clementine produced a derringer and held it in the palm of her hand. "Had those men presumed to touch me, I'd have used this."

Fargo took it. He'd seen the model before, a Remington pocket derringer, manufactured in various calibers. "Ma'am, this is a .17 caliber."

"I don't know what that means."

"It's good for shooting flies and mosquitoes but not much else."

"Nonsense. The man who sold it to me assured me I can drop a bear with that gun."

"The man who sold it to you was full of shit." Fargo handed the derringer back.

"I'll thank you to watch your language," Clementine said as her cannon disappeared into the folds of her dress.

"You shoot someone with that, it will only make them mad."

"You're patronizing me."

Fargo sighed.

"I've had to put up with that all my life," Clementine said. "You have no idea how hard it is for a woman to make her way in a man's world."

Her comment sparked Fargo's recollection of a female scout he'd known who felt the same, and how it brought about her end.

"I've shown them," Clementine said proudly. "I've shown everyone. I have an important position. I've proven how capable I am, and I demand the same respect a man would receive."

"Bodean and Judson were overflowing with respect," Fargo said.

"Why must you belittle me? They were callous brutes, and only interested in one thing."

"In other words," Fargo said, "they don't give a damn who you are."

Clementine broke stride, then resumed walking. "Oh," she said, as if surprised. "No, I suppose they don't, at that. And I can't come right out and tell them. We're supposed to keep our identity a secret."

"Do you think that's a good idea?"

"No," Clementine said. "I don't. But Washington does and they know best. Were I to go into the swamp under a military escort, with the major and his men in uniform, the Kilatku might see it as an act of war."

"So Washington sticks their soldiers in civilian clothes and have them pretend they're not."

They reached the woods and were enveloped in darkness.

Clementine moved closer, her shoulder brushing his. "Goodness. I can hardly see."

"I can," Fargo said.

"You must have eyes like a cat."

"Lots of practice." Fargo saw a log and took her hand.

She didn't object or yank free and he guided her around it and let go.

"I've been remiss. I should thank you for coming to my aid back there. Not that I needed any help, you understand."

Fargo grunted.

"You don't like me, do you?"

"Why wouldn't I?" Fargo said. "You have your nose up your ass but so do a lot of people."

"I resent that."

"You and the major."

"Are you suggesting we're alike, he and I?"

"He has his whole head up his ass."

"I wish you would stop being so crude," Clementine said, but she chuckled. "Although I suppose I deserved that for how I've treated you."

"Deserve has nothing to do with anything," Fargo said. "We are who we are."

"Listen to you." Clementine grinned. "You're quite the philosopher."

"Hell," Fargo said.

Clementine put a hand on his arm. "Will you be honest with me?"

"I have been so far."

"How do you rate our chances with the Kilatku? I very much need to succeed. My career may well depend on it."

"We'll be lucky to make it out alive."

6

"I didn't reckon on seein' you back so soon," Cotton said as Fargo bellied to the plank bar.

The saloon was crowded. Practically every man in Suttree's Landing was there for their nightly libation. A lot of those who lived in cabins off in the woods and a few brave souls who lived partway into the swamp were also wetting their throats.

"Whiskey," Fargo said. He'd left Clementine Purdy at the edge of the clearing. She'd seemed disappointed but he had business to take care of with a certain willing dove.

That, and he didn't care to get into another argument with Major Davenport.

Clementine had shot him a strange look as she'd strode from the trees. Fargo hadn't known what to make of it, and put it from his mind and hurried back, and now here he was—but no Sadie. He asked Cotton.

"She went into the back to see if I have another bottle of that damn sherry of hers. No one else drinks it. She thinks it makes her ladylike."

"I know a gent who drinks brandy because he thinks it makes his piss smell sweet."

"There's a heap of idiots in this world," Cotton opined. He indicated a hallway at the rear. "You're welcome to go see what's keepin' her."

The light penetrated only a short way. Fargo groped the wall until he came to a closed door with a glow at the bottom, and opened it.

A storage room contained a few shelves lined with bottles, many of them empty, plus several crates and containers. In a holder hanging from a peg, a candle flickered.

"Well, look who it is," Sadie said. She was seated on a crate, about to drink straight from a bottle of sherry. "You came back."

"Told you I would." Fargo shut the door. The room smelled of dust and spilled beer but it was warm and cozy.

"You're probably wonderin' what I'm doin' in here," Sadie said. She didn't wait for him to say whether he was or he wasn't. "I wanted a few minutes of peace and quiet to myself."

"You don't have peace and quiet at your own place?"

"Not with all the menfolk who stop by, no." Taking a long swig, Sadie smiled and held the bottle out. "Care for some?"

"Sherry?" Fargo said. "Maybe after I'm dead and buried."

Sadie laughed. "Don't tell me. You think sherry is for weak sisters."

"Or Easterners."

"Same difference," Sadie said. She patted a crate next to hers. "Have a seat, why don't you? It'll be a few minutes before I'm done."

Fargo made himself comfortable and propped his hands behind him. He looked around for a whiskey bottle but didn't see any.

"I don't have many restful moments like this," Sadie said. "Especially once the sun goes down." She swallowed more sherry. "Not that I have any regrets, mind you. I like what I do."

"Makes two of us," Fargo said. The last thing he needed was a dove in her cups who felt sorry for herself. He could do without the tears.

"Do you know why I live here instead of somewhere like New Orleans?"

A talker, Fargo thought, and smothered a frown. "I reckon you'll tell me."

"Life is slower here. And the men are mostly bumpkins

I can wrap around my finger." Sadie smiled sort of sadly. "I'm the queen of Suttree's Landin', and that beats bein' just another whore somewhere else."

Fargo admired the swell of her breasts and how her dress draped over her thighs.

"What is it a man told me once? A big fish in a small pond is better than bein' a small fish in a big pond. He had it exactly right."

Fargo liked how her ruby lips glued to the mouth of the sherry bottle. He imagined them glued to his.

"It's not as if bein' a dove was my life's ambition or anything. When I was little, I didn't look in a mirror and say to myself, 'I'll make a fine whore one day.'"

"Hell," Fargo said.

"What? Am I too maudlin? I've been told I get that way on occasion."

Her smooth neck, ripe for licking, her thin waist, ready for his hands to wrap around; Fargo could put up with maudlin for a bit.

"Do you know what my plan is?" Sadie asked, and answered her own question. "I aim to stick around another ten years or so. I'll save practically every cent I make, and about the time my looks start to go, I'm off to a city to live like a proper lady."

"Your looks will last longer than ten years."

"What a sweet thing to say." Sadie reached over and pressed her palm to his cheek. "God, you are man-candy. I get wet just looking at you."

Fargo was off the crate in the blink of an eye. "Do you, now?" He stood in front of her, cupped her chin, and kissed her, lightly.

"I can't wait for later," Sadie said throatily.

"Who says we have to?"

Sadie blinked, and gazed about them. "Here? You can't be serious."

"There's room," Fargo said, with a nod at the dirt floor.

"And muss my dress? Not on your life."

"Fine," Fargo said, and placing his hands on either side of her waist, he pulled her off the crate so she was flush against him.

"Feeling randy, are we?" Sadie teased.

"Put the bottle down."

Sadie turned and set the sherry on the crate. Then, smiling innocently, she batted her eyelids and said, "Why, good sir, whatever do you have in mind?"

"I am to do you, ma'am."

"Do little ol' me?" Sadie went on playing. "Just be careful. Rip my dress and you'll buy me a new one."

"And if I bite off a tit?"

Sadie giggled. "Why, sugar. That would take a lot of bitin'. Mine are each about the size of the moon."

Fargo snorted. "They're big but they're not that damn big."

"Why don't you pretend I'm a corncob and this dress is the husk and peel it off and find out just how huge they are."

Fargo's groin was tingling. He kissed her again, harder this time, and rimmed her soft lips with his tongue.

He cupped a breast and squeezed, and his pole surged.

Sadie placed her hand on his bulge. "Oh my," she said in his ear. "What do we have here? There's a tree in your pants. And it's rock hard."

"Hussy," Fargo said.

"And proud of it, I'll have you know. Lucky for you, too. Were I a church-going lady, I'd hit you with a bottle along about now."

Fargo kissed her mouth, her cheeks, her throat, all the while caressing her body with one hand and prying at her buttons and stays with the other. She knew to make it easy for the men, and thankfully, after only a dozen buttons, her dress was open enough that he could slide it off her shoulders, exposing her chemise.

"My, oh my," she went on teasing. "You must have done this before."

"Once or twice," Fargo growled.

"Fibber," Sadie said. "Somethin' tells me you have to fight the ladies off with a stick."

"I never fight a lady off," Fargo said. Not when they were willing and wanton and wanted it as much as he did.

"And I never say no to a payin' customer," Sadie said. "Which reminds me. Usually I ask for the money in advance."

Fargo started to reach for his poke but she placed her hand on his wrist.

"In your case I'll make an exception."

"Awful nice of you."

"Like I said, you're easy on the eyes. And you don't stink to high heaven, like those who think that takin' a bath is bad for the health."

Fargo grunted. His nose was assaulted by the stink of the unwashed practically every day. "You smell real nice, like a flower."

"Flattery, dear sir," Sadie grinned, "will get you everywhere."

"Then let's shut the hell up and get to it."

Placing his hands on her bottom, Fargo lifted her off the ground.

"What in the world?" Sadie blurted.

Turning, Fargo carried her to a clear space along a wall and pressed her against it and set her down.

"Oh." Sadie chuckled. "I get it. You aim to have me standin' up."

"Unless you want to try it standing on our heads," Fargo said.

Sadie chortled. "That is one way I haven't. Well, that, and on top of a kitchen table, which I've always hankered to do."

Fargo silenced her with his mouth. Their hands were everywhere, exploring, massaging, stoking, stroking. Presently his pants were down around his ankles and her dress was up around her waist.

Sadie ground against him and said throatily, "I want you so much."

"I bet you say that to all the gents."

"No, you jackass, I don't," Sadie said, and fiercely kissed him.

Fargo was about to part her legs and penetrate her when he heard the storeroom door open.

"Sadie? Mister?" Cotton said. "What's keepin' you two so—" He stopped in his tracks. "Oh shit," he exclaimed, and slammed the door shut again. "You better not break anything!"

"Goodness gracious," Sadie said. "We must have shocked him."

"I doubt it," Fargo said. "He'd probably stay and watch if he wasn't afraid I'd shoot him."

"Would you?"

"Hell yes. I don't need an audience."

Sadie laughed and nipped his neck. "I do so admire a man who knows his own pecker."

Fargo placed a hand on her knee, slid it up her inner thigh to her bushy thatch, and parted her nether lips.

"How do you feel about a man who likes to fuck?"

"Need you ask, silly goose?"

He rammed up into her and she gasped and arched her back. Her legs rose and she locked her ankles at the small of his back.

"Keep goin'!" Sadie husked.

Fargo did. He drove up and in, over and over, moving faster and harder. Sadie matched his thrusts with the rhythm of her pelvis. She panted and clawed and tried to suck his mouth into hers. Suddenly she gave a low cry, and spurted. It triggered his own.

Afterward, as they sagged against one another, spent and breathless, Sadie giggled and nibbled his earlobe.

"I've taken a shine to you, handsome. There's no charge for the poke."

"In that case," Fargo said, covering her tits with his hands, "how about a second helping?"

"Oh my," Sadie said.

7

"You look like something the cat dragged in," Sergeant Morgan remarked, a rare smile creasing his stony countenance.

Fargo grunted as he poured steaming coffee into his tin cup.

"Are those scratch marks on your neck?"

"A tree limb poked me."

"Did the tree limb suck on your throat and leave that red mark, too?" Morgan chuckled and walked toward the horses.

"Funny hombre," Fargo said, and took a sip. God, he needed it. Sadie hadn't been content with seconds; she'd craved a third helping of his redwood. When it came to lovemaking, that gal was a bottomless well of desire. Insatiable, was how those who liked big words would describe her. She had just about fucked his brains out.

He grinned at the thought.

"Something has you in fine spirits," Clementine Purdy commented as she took a seat across the fire. "Good morning, by the way."

Fargo grunted.

"What time did you get in?"

"That's your business how?" Fargo wasn't about to mention that it had been about three a.m.

"I take it back," Clementine said. "You're not in fine fettle. You're prickly."

Major Davenport appeared, scrubbed and shaved and as ramrod straight as ever. "I see you made it back," he said sarcastically.

Fargo tried to ignore him.

"Did you find out anything about that surveyor, Williams, and his people?"

"Nothing new."

"I told you that you'd be wasting your time."

"I wouldn't say that," Fargo said.

Davenport gazed in the direction of Suttree's Landing. "With any luck, one of the locals will volunteer to be our guide and we'll be able to rent the extra boats we need and get under way."

"Into the heart of the Archaletta Swamp," Clementine said excitedly. "It promises to be quite an adventure."

"That it will, dear lady," Davenport said, "and a feather in both our caps."

"Provided we make it back here in one piece," Fargo couldn't resist reminding them.

"We will," Davenport confidently predicted. "Williams was a civilian. So were his helpers." He gestured at Morgan and the four troopers. "We're military. We're professionals. The savages won't find us anywhere near as easy to slay."

"You ever hear of a duck out of water?"

In the act of bending to grip the coffeepot, Davenport paused. "Are you suggesting we're out of our element? We'll have boats. We're armed with the latest rifles and revolvers. The Kilatku use knives and clubs, I understand. They don't even have bows and arrows." Davenport shook his head. "No, swamp or no swamp, we have every advantage. I dare say we can hold their entire tribe at bay."

Fargo's mood went from prickly to sour; overconfidence killed more men than stupidity. "I won't say you don't know what in hell you're talking about," he said, "but you don't know what in hell you're talking about."

"I warned you before about the tone you take with me."

"Major"—Fargo curbed his temper—"the Kilatku have lived in the swamp since before the Pilgrims came over from

England. They know it inside and out. And their knives and clubs can kill as easy as our rifles and revolvers."

"Only if they can get close enough to use them," Davenport said. "We won't let them."

"The seven of us," Fargo said.

"Each of us has a Henry rifle," Davenport said, "each of which holds fifteen rounds. Sixteen, if there's a cartridge in the chamber when we load the magazine. Do the arithmetic. That's over one hundred shots we can fire before we have to reload. And from what we've gleaned, there aren't more than forty or fifty warriors in the whole tribe."

"You have it all worked out," Clementine complimented him.

"Indeed I do, my dear," Davenport boasted. "I was at the top of my class in military strategy at West Point."

Fargo sighed.

"What?" Davenport said.

"Book learning and drilling on a parade ground don't make you a match for the Kilatku."

"Honestly," Davenport said in undisguised scorn, "I'm beginning to wonder why the general felt you would be of any use. Your attitude leaves considerable to be desired."

And yours, Fargo wanted to say but didn't, could get all of us killed.

Davenport smiled at Clementine. "You need not worry in the least, Miss Purdy. My men and I will ensure you accomplish your mission and return safely."

"Thank you, Major."

Morgan walked up, stood at attention, and saluted. "We're ready to move out, sir, whenever you give the word."

"Thank you, Sergeant," Davenport said. "But remember. We're not to let anyone know who we are. The Kilatku might not meet with us if they suspect we're soldiers. Kindly refrain from saluting until I say otherwise."

"Yes, sir. Sorry, sir."

Fargo almost laughed. Not saluting wasn't enough to hide the fact they were soldiers given that the major and his men conducted themselves exactly as they would were they in uniform.

Not twenty minutes later they were on their horses, headed for the settlement.

Fargo came last, and was mildly surprised when Clementine Purdy reined around and brought her sorrel alongside the Ovaro.

"Do you mind if I ask you a question?"

"A tree limb poked me," Fargo said.

"What? No. I saw your face when the major was talking. You don't share his confidence, do you?"

"That's putting it mildly."

"Is it because you consider the Kilatku to be more formidable than he does?"

"It's because they're not all we have to worry about."

Clementine was silent until they emerged from the woods. "What else is there?"

Fargo reminded himself she was from the East, and pointed at the morass of water and vegetation beyond the hamlet. "The swamp. It's as much an enemy as the Kilatku."

"But we have more than ample provisions. And in our boats we'll be perfectly safe."

"Tell that to Williams and his men."

"Why must you be so cynical about everything?" Clementine bit her lower lip. "But Uncle Thomas did say I could trust you. I'm counting on you to watch over me once we're in the swamp."

"That's why I'm here."

"I don't share your cynicism, I'll have you know. And if we make it back without mishap, I'll be temped to rub your nose in it."

Fargo stared at her bosom. "I know what I'd like to rub my nose in."

Clementine's mouth fell. "You can't mean what I think you mean."

"I don't mean your hair."

A scarlet tinge spread from her neckline to her hairline. "You, sir, are a rogue."

"No," Fargo said. "I'm just randy."

"I don't know what to think of you," Clementine said angrily. "I'll remind you that you should be on your best behavior or I'll tell my uncle." With that, she jabbed her heels and rode on ahead.

Suttree's Landing was astir. The general store was being opened and floors were being swept and a woman was taking down clothes she had left on a line all night. Over at the water, several fishermen were preparing to venture out.

After his clash with Bodean, Judson and Cleon, Fargo reckoned that was the last he would see of them. He was wrong.

The trio were waiting out front of the saloon. Bodean and Judson smirked like cats about to pounce on canaries. Cleon was trying to chew his lip off.

"Mr. Davenport," Bodean said in greeting. "We're here bright and early like you wanted."

The major leaned on his saddle horn. "I commend your punctuality."

"Our what?" Judson said.

Davenport looked around. "Where's the guide I asked for? And what about the boats we need?"

Bodean's oily smile was suspicious in itself but the major didn't seem to notice. "We've done talked it over, Jud and me, and we figure to guide you ourselves. Cleon ain't made up his mind whether he'll come or not."

"You and your friend have been deep into the swamp?" Davenport asked.

"Hell, we've been all over the Archaletta," Bodean boasted. "No one knows it better than we do."

Fargo brought the Ovaro up next to the major. "He's lying."

"Like hell I am," Bodean bristled.

Major Davenport said, "On what grounds, Mr. Fargo, do you make your accusation? It seems to me they are exactly who we need."

"They're doing it to get back at me," Fargo explained. "We had a run-in last night."

"Get back at you how?"

"How the hell would I know," Fargo said. "The important thing is that you can't trust them as far as you can throw your horse."

Major Davenport faced the swamp rats. "Can I, gentlemen? Trust you?"

"As God is my witness," Bodean said, placing his hand over his heart. "Our fight with him has nothin' to do with this."

"May the Almighty strike us dead if it does," Judson chimed in.

"We can use the money," Bodean went on. "Although, now that I think of it, you ain't said how much you're willin' to pay."

"A hundred dollars," Davenport said. "Fifty to each of you."

"That's more than we've seen in a coon's age," Judson said.

"Hell, it's more than most folks hereabouts earn in a year," Bodean said. "We accept."

"Then you're hired," Davenport said.

Fargo barely contained his disgust. People like Davenport were born without any common sense and got dumber as they got older.

"We thank you, mister," Bodean was saying to the major. "And to further show there are no hard feelin's, we'll let you use our own boats."

"Mine is a big one," Judson said. "It can hold a heap of supplies."

"Did you hear that?" Davenport said to Fargo. "Everything is working out exactly as I'd hoped. We have our guides and we have our craft." He gazed down the street at the landing and the vast uncharted wilds beyond.

"That swamp is as good as vanquished."

8

The Archaletta Swamp. Hundreds of square miles of brackish water that on hot days assaulted the nose. Water so dark, alligators could lurk just below the surface and you wouldn't know it. Bogs were common, quicksand a peril. Dismal, dank, with stretches of mossy forest and occasional hummocks and islands, the swamp crawled with snakes.

Flies were a daytime plague. Mosquitoes were legion after the sun went down. A chorus of frogs filled the humid air at night, broken now and again by the bellows of gators.

Leeches lurked in the pools and inlets; an arm or leg carelessly submerged too long would be covered with them.

Rank vegetation grew where it could. At times it was so thick, a man couldn't see ten feet in any direction.

Briars snagged the unwary. Reeds hid cottonmouths.

While Fargo loved the mountains and could never get enough of the prairie, he wasn't fond of swamps. They were death traps. Fang and claw ruled, and woe to any fool who let his or her guard down for even an instant.

Now, hunkered in the second boat, stroking his paddle smoothly, Fargo wished he'd said no when the general asked him to look after Clementine.

In the first boat Major Davenport was consulting a map and a compass. Bodean was beside him. Sergeant Morgan and Judson were paddling.

The last two boats carried two soldiers apiece, and the packs and everything else they'd brought.

"This heat is abominable," Clementine remarked. "I don't know how anyone can stand it."

Fargo prayed she wouldn't talk his ears off again. Gabby women were one of his peeves. He shared the boat with her and Cleon, who chose that moment to clear his throat.

"A body gets used to the hot after a while, ma'am. Those of us born here don't hardly notice it."

"I don't see how," Clementine said.

A startled heron took wing and a frightened frog made a loud splash.

Clementine bent to peer over the side, and gasped.

"Did you see that? Either of you?"

"See what, ma'am?" Cleon asked.

"I swear I saw a snake with a fish in its mouth."

"You probably did," Cleon said. "Snakes eat whatever they can catch. Most will leave you be. It's the ones that want to sink their poison into you that you have to watch out for."

"I'm afraid I'm rather squeamish when it comes to snakes," Clementine said.

"Don't touch anything that wriggles and you should be fine," Cleon cautioned her.

"Have you nothing to say on the subject, Mr. Fargo?" Clementine said.

"The deeper in we go, the more snakes there will be."

"How wonderful of you to point that out."

"He's just tryin' to be helpful, ma'am," Cleon said.

"On the contrary," Clementine said. "He's reminding me, yet again, that I shouldn't be here."

Fargo was doing his best to memorize landmarks. He had a knack for it that in part accounted for his success as a scout. It was strange how he could forget the name of someone he met, but he never forgot a butte or a bluff or the lay of terrain. On dry land, anyhow. In a swamp the landmarks were few. One cypress tree looked pretty much like the next, one thicket little different from its neighbor, one pool much like every other pool.

Out of the blue Cleon asked, "When do you reckon the shootin' will commence?"

"Shooting?" Clementine absently responded.

"Yes, ma'am. Shootin' the gators. That's why Mr. Davenport is here, ain't it?"

"Oh. Yes. Of course." Clementine fiddled with her bonnet. "I've heard him say he wants a large one for his trophy room. None of those we've seen so far have been all that big."

"The big ones mostly come out at night," Cleon informed her. "They're hard to spot, let alone shoot."

"I have every confidence in Mr. Davenport," Clementine said.

"I'm surprised he didn't bring a fancy sportin' rifle," Cleon said. "That Henry he carries won't do him much good on the really big gators."

"He told me it can drop a buffalo."

"I wouldn't know about buffs. I know gators. Their hides are awful thick. His Henry might do no more than tickle 'em."

"You should talk to Mr. Davenport about it," Clementine said. "He's the hunter."

"And what are you, ma'am, if you don't mind my askin'? His sweetheart?"

"I'm . . . an acquaintance," Clementine hedged.

"That's all? Yet you let him drag you out here to be bit by a water moccasin or drowned or maybe be jumped by a bunch of hostiles?"

Clementine fluffed with her collar. "That will be quite enough of that kind of talk."

"What kind, ma'am?"

"Dying talk."

"If'n you don't like to think about death," Cleon said, "you shouldn't ought to be here."

That was all any of them said until they had gone another quarter of a mile and came to a narrow channel of clear water.

"It looks so inviting," Clementine said, dipping her fingers in.

"I wouldn't do that were I you," Cleon said. "A gator once bit my cousin's hand clean off."

The sun was low on the western horizon and Fargo's shoulders were aching when Davenport veered toward a grass-topped hummock that was high enough to spare them from the worst of the bugs and to reduce the risk of a prowling gator invading their camp.

Morgan and his men went about setting up while Bodean, Judson and Cleon went to collect firewood.

Davenport came over to where Fargo was filling a coffee-pot with water while Clementine hovered. "So far, so good," he said, sounding pleased with himself.

"It's been one day," Fargo said.

"Without incident, I must point out."

"In a couple more we'll be so far in, we couldn't send for help if we wanted to," Fargo mentioned.

Davenport patted his Henry. "These are all the help we'll need."

A corporal by the name of Harris did the cooking. Afterward, the soldiers sat in one group and their escorts in another, and smoked and talked.

Fargo sat apart from everyone else, nursing his last coffee of the day. He wasn't alone long.

"Mind if I join you?" Clementine roosted and wrapped her arms around her knees.

"You look annoyed," Fargo noted.

Clementine frowned. "The major is being too protective. He won't let me out of his sight."

"I reckon he thinks he's doing his duty."

"Even so," Clementine said, "when I went off into the bushes, he wanted to send one of his men with me. Can you imagine."

Fargo grinned. "I wouldn't mind holding your hand."

"I very much doubt that's all you'd try to hold," Clementine said. "Let's be perfectly clear. There will be none of *that* out here."

"That?" Fargo said innocently.

"I've seen how you look at me. As if you'd like to eat me alive."

"The Kilatku are the cannibals," Fargo said. "Or so folks say."

Clementine peered into the ink of night that surrounded their lone bastion of light. From out of it came a cacophony of sounds; the chirp and buzz of insects, the croaking of scores of frogs, the growls and roars of alligators. From way off came the piercing screech of a bobcat. "Did you hear that?"

"My ears work fine."

Clementine shuddered. "It's unnerving, I must confess."

Fargo felt compelled to say, "It's not too late to turn back."

"I couldn't if I wanted to. Our government is counting on me. And I've explained how important this is to my career."

"No career is worth dying over."

"Honestly," Clementine said. "You act as if we're all doomed."

Fargo was spared from having to reply by Cleon, who sank down with his chin in his hands. "Howdy, folks," he said gloomily.

"What's wrong?" Clementine asked.

"Nothin', ma'am," Cleon said. "Just wanted some different company."

"Aren't you and your friends getting along?"

"Them and me don't always see eye to eye," Cleon said. "I told them I didn't want to guide you but they offered to anyway."

"We couldn't find the Kilatku without your help," Clementine said.

"You're askin' for trouble," Cleon said. "We should turn back while we can."

"Not you, too? Mr. Fargo just said the very same thing."

Cleon nodded at Fargo. "We're the only two who admit the truth."

"Are you worried about the Kilatku?"

"Them, and a lot more besides." Cleon gazed out across the benighted domain of a thousand-and-one deaths. "I'm not just talkin' about gators and such. There's other things out here. Things we're not meant to set eyes on."

"What on earth are you talking about?"

Cleon bent toward her. "There's an old witchy woman who lives out here somewhere. She comes into the Landing now and again but no one has anything to do with her. Once she got mad at Abe Tyler for some reason or another and put a curse on him, and within a week he was dead."

"That's preposterous."

"Then there's the ghost. Some have seen it late at night, glidin' over the waters. They say if it touches you, it freezes your blood."

"Really now," Clementine said. "Are we children who believe in fairy tales?"

"The ghost ain't no fairy, ma'am. It's a spook. And it ain't the only one. There's other things. Like the skunk apes. They get hold of you, they'll tear you limb from limb."

"Enough is enough," Clementine said. "If you're trying to scare me, it won't work. I don't believe in witches or ghosts or your ridiculous apes. There are no such things."

"You don't have to believe in them for them to kill you, ma'am."

"I refuse to listen to any more of this nonsense," Clementine declared.

Cleon sadly shook his head and said to Fargo. "We are in for it, ain't we?"

"We sure as hell are."

9

As if to prove Fargo wrong, the next several days were not just uneventful, they were downright peaceful. The skies were sunny and dispelled much of the swamp's natural gloom.

They saw a dozen or so alligators, mostly small, none of which came anywhere near. The few snakes they spotted slithered quickly away.

Bodean and Judson proved as good as their word; they piloted the boats along a network of channels unmarred by bogs and quicksand.

By the evening of the fourth day the soldiers were much less alert. Even Major Davenport had relaxed a bit and joked with his men around the campfire.

Fargo regarded it as the lull before the storm. He knew swamps, had been in them before, and each time barely survived to make it out again.

Someone shared his sentiment. Cleon had taken to sitting with him at night, and flapped his gums nonstop.

Fargo learned more about the Archaletta than he ever wanted to know. He learned a lot about Suttree's Landing, too, and the people who called it home. People who lived in fear of the swamp they lived next to. People who wouldn't venture where they were going for all the gold ever dug out of the ground.

"Tomorrow it gets worse," Cleon informed him. "We run out of good water. It'll be mostly pure swamp from then on."

"We haven't seen a single Indian yet," Fargo mentioned.

"The friendly ones, those as come to trade, don't know you," Cleon said. "To them you're strangers. They're out there, though, watchin'." He poked at his teeth with a sliver he was using as a toothpick. "Get a good night's sleep, friend. You'll need it."

Fargo took him up on it and turned in early. He thought of the Ovaro, in Cotton's care until he returned, and wished he had the stallion under him instead of a flat-bottom boat. The crafts were slow and ponderous. They were especially hard to turn quickly if the need arose. He'd rather they used canoes but it would take a dozen to hold all of them and their supplies.

Fargo slept soundly, as he nearly always did in the wilds. He woke only once, when a panther shrieked like a woman in labor.

Daybreak brought a pall of gloom. Gray clouds had scuttled in, suggesting it would rain before the day was done.

They set out as usual, the major and the sergeant in the first boat, Fargo in the second with Clementine and Cleon, the rest after.

The channel they'd been following merged into a murky expanse of still water towered over by ranks of moss-caked cypress.

For a while an oppressive silence fell. The birds stopped warbling. The insects stopped buzzing.

"Why is it so quiet?" Clementine whispered.

"It gets that way when there are hostiles about," Cleon said, "or worse."

Fargo dipped his paddle and strained his senses. He caught movement and spotted an alligator breaking the surface a stone's throw away.

"God in heaven," Clementine breathed.

Ten feet from the tip of its nose to the end of its tail, the beast's unblinking eyes regarded them as if it were trying to decide if they were edible.

"Shucks, ma'am," Cleon said, "that's not even one of the big ones."

The cypress seemed to go on forever but it was only an hour later that they wound into a maze where the water was hemmed by thickets and brush. At times the vegetation formed a bower over their heads.

"I don't like this," Clementine nervously complained. "Anything could jump out at us."

It didn't help that the undergrowth was infested with snakes. Fargo would see them entwined in the branches, or slithering, or a head would appear and a tongue flick at them.

The boat was passing under an arch of limbs when Clementine suddenly screamed and pushed to her feet, causing the whole boat to tilt and Fargo to nearly lose his balance.

Something was around her neck and across her shoulders, and she smacked at it and shrieked.

Cleon started to rise but Fargo reached her first. He grabbed the snake behind its head, tore it off her, and threw it into the water.

"It bit me!" Clementine cried, pressing a hand to her neck. She put her other hand to her brow, and swayed.

Fargo caught her before she swooned. He eased her down to her seat and held her as she quaked. Moving her hand aside, he examined the wound. The bite hadn't broken her skin.

"You're all right, ma'am," Cleon said, taking her other hand and patting it. "That was a yellow-bellied water snake. They're not poisonous."

"God," Clementine said, and clutched at Fargo's shoulders.

Up in the first boat, Major Davenport hollered, "Is Miss Purdy all right?"

"Give her a minute," Fargo yelled. He cupped her chin and smiled. "You were lucky."

"God," she said again.

"I remember one time a water moccasin fell on me," Cleon said. "Bit at me, too, but only got my hat. I tore it off and went at it with my knife. Must have chopped it into a hundred pieces or more, and then I just sat there shakin' like a leaf."

"Is that supposed to cheer me up?" Clementine asked.

"Sort of," Cleon said.

Despite the heat and the humidity, Clementine took out a shawl and wrapped it around her shoulders and neck.

Eventually the thickets gave way to murky water dotted by hummocks and islands and strips of land covered by impenetrable tangles.

The clouds darkened and a breeze kicked up and brought a familiar scent.

"It'll rain soon," Cleon said to them. Then he shouted, "Bodean! The rain!"

"I have eyes and a nose," the other swamp man shot back. "We can beat it to Split Skull Island."

"Not there, of all places," Cleon said, to himself rather than to them.

Clementine roused to say, "Split Skull Island? I've never heard of it."

"Only us locals have," Cleon said. "It's as far in as most of us have come."

"Why Split Skull?" Fargo wanted to know.

"You'll see soon enough."

The speed of the first boat increased.

Fargo and Cleon kept pace. They skirted a vile-appearing bog, crossed a short belt of open water, and approached an island.

Bodean and Judson turned their boat and hugged the shoreline until they came to an inlet. Nosing in, they scraped their boat to a stop on a gravel bar.

Fargo followed suit.

The wind was a lot stronger, the clouds writhed and twisted.

"There's a shack," Bodean said, pointing up a well-worn path. "It's not much but it's better than being soaked to the skin."

Once the boats were secure, Davenport barked commands and Morgan and the troopers set to work toting the packs inland.

Fargo helped Clementine carry her things. The trail was as sinuous as the snakes they'd been seeing. Eventually it brought them to a clearing. In the middle stood a sorry excuse for shelter. One wall had partially caved in and there was no door and only tatters of burlap over the window.

"Goodness," Clementine said, her nose crinkling. "What's that terrible smell?"

"Maybe a dead swamp rat," Cleon said. "They're a powerful nuisance."

Sure enough, Fargo noticed a dead one in a corner. Someone had skewered it with a blade and left it to rot.

Three trips, and everything was in the shack. The soldiers got a fire going.

Clementine sat with Davenport and Morgan, Cleon with his friends.

Left to himself, Fargo went back out. He made a circuit of the shack and the clearing. On the east side, at a patch of bare earth, he drew up short at the sight of moccasin prints, a whole one and a heel. Fresh, too.

He wondered if the Indians had heard them coming and retreated into the undergrowth. Leveling the Henry, he went in after them.

A mosquito buzzed his face. Another alighted on his sleeve.

Moving as silently as an Apache, Fargo avoided briars, slipped over a log, padded through waist-high grass. Another partial print pointed to the right.

Fargo slowed. He hadn't seen or heard anything but he had a feeling he wasn't alone. Someone—or something—was watching him.

Surrounded by a green and brown cocoon, he cautiously crabbed forward.

Fargo didn't know what made him stop. He scoured the shadows, scouted them a second time, and stiffened, his skin crawling.

Twenty feet away a pair of dark eyes were fixed on him with fierce intensity. He couldn't see the face. He started forward and the eyes disappeared. Unfurling, he crashed through the undergrowth but when he got to where the eyes had been, he saw no one, heard nothing.

Fargo dropped to a knee, the Henry to his cheek. It had to be an Indian. Whether friendly or hostile, he couldn't say.

A minute dragged into two and two into five and nothing happened. Either the Indian had fled or gone to ground and was waiting for him to leave.

Reluctantly, Fargo did. It wouldn't be smart to blunder around. Retracing his steps to the clearing, he lowered the Henry and stopped for a last look back.

The eyes were there again, about the same distance as before.

Fargo broke out in gooseflesh. He hadn't heard a sound. The owner of those eyes was as silent as the specters the swampers feared.

"There you are!"

Fargo gave a start, and turned. Clementine was coming toward him. He glanced back at the eyes but they weren't there. Moving to intercept her, he grasped her arm. "Far enough."

"What's the matter?"

"Company," Fargo said, with a bob of his head at the plant life run riot.

"Someone from Suttree's Landing?" Clementine asked.

"More likely trouble," Fargo said. "And soon."

10

When Cleon said the next day would be worse, he wasn't kidding.

The swamp underwent a change. Where before there had been spots of clear water and tracts of dry land, now the Archaletta was everything a swamp was notorious for being; a noxious quagmire of perpetual bogs and quicksand and treacherous waterways for navigation.

The vegetation changed, too. It was ranker, darker, thicker. Loathsome growth that made the skin crawl to look at it.

Insects swarmed in clouds that plagued them incessantly.

Strangely, there were fewer snakes, but those they saw were larger. Clementine let out a cry of horror at a giant that had to be fifteen feet long, sunning itself on a log.

A bulge in its middle was all that was left of recent prey.

It paid no attention as they glided by.

Alligators thrived. Where before they'd see one or two over the span of an hour, now they saw dozens. Some were enormous, virtual monsters that stared at their passing craft without fear.

Small wonder, then, Major Davenport called them all together around the fire that evening and began with, "From here on out, everyone is to stay on their guard every moment."

"As if we wouldn't," Cleon said.

Davenport scowled and continued. "I fear we've failed to fully appreciate how dangerous this swamp can be."

"We tried to warn you, mister," Bodean piped up. "But you knew better than us who have lived here all our lives."

Judson nodded.

"Be that as it may," Davenport said testily, "I'm beginning to wonder if these ventures are unwise."

Clementine sat up. "How can you say that? Our superiors think it's necessary."

Fargo saw Davenport stiffen at her blunder. He also saw Bodean and Judson glance at one another, as if their suspicions were confirmed.

"We're here to hunt, remember?" Davenport said. "I was referring to anyone who might have penetrated this far previously. It could be that they met their end in any number of ways."

Fargo realized what the major was getting at. Maybe the Kilatku hadn't killed the surveyor and his party. Maybe the swamp killed them.

Clementine, though, had so forgotten herself that she said, "We're under orders, and I, for one, intend to carry those orders out."

"Orders, ma'am?" Cleon said.

Clementine blinked, and blushed, and started to stammer a reply.

"We thought so," Bodean cut her off. "Gator hunters my ass."

"You folks are here for some other reason," Judson declared.

"For the government," Bodean said. "Pokin' its nose in where it don't belong."

Major Davenport frowned, then nodded. "Very well. Since Miss Purdy has let the cat out of the bag, it's to our mutual benefit for me to reveal the truth. Yes, we were sent by Washington. We're to try and establish peaceful relations with the Kilatku so the swamp can be surveyed."

Bodean laughed. "Of all the harebrained notions, that takes the cake."

"It's a *swamp*, for God's sake," Judson said. "Why in hell survey it?"

Sergeant Morgan stirred to say, "Watch your language around Miss Purdy."

Judson glared at him and went to say something but apparently changed his mind.

"Listen, you men," Davenport said to the swampers. "You're doing our country a great service by helping us carry out our mission. To you this is nothing but worthless swamp, and truth to tell, personally, I agree. But the government wants it surveyed. It's important that every square foot of this country of ours be mapped end to end."

"Important to idiots, maybe," Bodean said. "Not to us."

"To the damn politicians," Judson said.

"Same thing," Bodean replied.

Clementine jabbed a finger at them. "Honestly, you two. Aren't you patriotic? Where's your sense of duty to your country?"

"I left it in my long underwear back at the Landing," Bodean said.

Judson pointed a finger at her. "Lady, if the redcoats were invadin' again, we'd be first in line to fight. But we're riskin' our hides so some highbrow can put a bunch of squiggles on a piece of paper."

"The government thinks the maps are important."

"What has my goat," Bodean said, "is that you lied to us."

"Under orders," Clementine said.

Davenport came to her defense with, "Yes, I admit we deceived you, but only in the best interests of our country."

Cleon cleared his throat. "I don't hold the lyin' against you all that much. I don't like it none, but what's done is done." He studied the major and Clementine. "What's more important is whether you folks aim to go through with this?"

"Of course," Davenport said.

"Then you're plumb crazy. Not two minutes ago you told

us you can see why anyone who comes this far in winds up dead. Now you want us dead, too?"

"We're prepared for anything," Major Davenport assured him.

"No, mister, you're not. You only think you are. I'm warnin' you folks for the last time. Turn around before it's too late."

"We can't."

Cleon looked at Fargo as if expecting him to take his side.

"I don't have a say," Fargo said.

They were camped on a strip of dry land with an odious bog to their left and a stagnant pool to their right. Just then a tremendous splash caused the pool to roil and brought all of them to their feet, the men with their rifles raised.

"What in hell?" Judson blurted.

Bending, Fargo gripped the unlit end of a brand, raised it over his head, and took a few steps toward the pool. He didn't get too close, just enough that he saw ripples where something enormous had sunk below the surface.

"A gator," Bodean said. "Had to be."

"You hope," Cleon said.

"What else?" Bodean asked.

"Who knows what's out here," Cleon said. "You've heard the tales the same as me."

"Enough," Major Davenport said. "You're scaring Miss Purdy."

Clementine had her hand to her throat, her eyes wide as saucers. "I never imagined . . . ," she said, and let it go at that.

Fargo suspected the truth was beginning to dawn. She'd had it in her head that the swamp couldn't possibly be as dangerous as everyone claimed. She'd figured to waltz in, meet with the Kilatku and win them over, and waltz out again, suffering no more inconvenience than a few mosquito bites. Now it was sinking in that it wouldn't be as easy as she thought; at any time, anything could happen. He almost felt sorry for her.

"Whatever it was, it didn't attack," Davenport said. "You can relax."

"Can I?" Clementine said.

"My men will take turns keeping watch. The rest of you can turn in."

"We don't mind takin' a turn," Bodean offered.

"That's right," Judson said. "We'll do our part."

"I thank you but it's not necessary," Davenport told them.

Fargo had trouble getting to sleep. The previous nights couldn't begin to compare to this one. On all sides rose a riotous bedlam of roars and shrieks and screams, so many and so loud, the very air seemed to pulse to the savage beat. It didn't help that from nearby came furtive rustling and slitherings.

Along about the middle of the night he dozed off and slept fitfully until just before dawn. He was the first up save for the man on guard, who nodded.

Everyone was in a mood to match the swamp. After a hasty breakfast, they packed up and moved to the boats.

The same trooper who had been last on sentry duty stepped to the rope that secured one and stooped to unfasten it.

The water exploded. Out of it hurtled a reptilian behemoth, its jaws spread wide. Before the trooper could recoil or cry out, the alligator's mouth clamped shut with awful force. Bones cracked and blood spurted, and the next instant the gator was hauling its quarry back into the water.

It happened so fast, everyone was rooted in shock.

Fargo recovered first, and snapping the Henry to his shoulder, he took a hasty bead between the alligator's eyes. He thumbed back the hammer—and the gator went under.

"Private Baker!" Morgan cried, and took a stride toward the pool.

"No!" Davenport shouted, grabbing the sergeant by the arm. "There's nothing you can do."

Morgan tried to pull free, then stopped and said, aghast, "He didn't stand a chance."

"I've been tryin' to warn you," Cleon said.

"The alligator is gone and will be busy for a while," Davenport said. He didn't elaborate on what it would be doing. "Let's finish loading and get under way."

One boat after the other, they pushed off and glided along a blue-green ribbon that wound deeper into the foreboding heart of the Archaletta.

"Did you see that poor man?" Clementine said softly. "The look on his face."

"It was over fast," Cleon said, dipping his paddle. "I doubt he suffered much."

"That could have been any of us." Clementine stared out over the swamp with horror writ on her face. "If I'd only known, I'd never have agreed to come." Stark fear replaced the horror.

"Stay calm, ma'am," Cleon said. "It won't do to lose your head."

"What have I let myself in for?" Clementine asked herself.

"It could be, ma'am," Cleon said, "we're all in for an early grave."

Fargo was going to tell him not to scare her more than she already was, but the hell of it was, Cleon was right.

11

Their boats moved through a gray world of dim shapes and furtive sounds. Not so much as a single shaft of sunlight broke through the clouds.

Sergeant Morgan was in the last boat, teamed with the trooper whose partner had perished.

Bodean and Judson handled the first boat. Major Davenport sat with his nose to something he was reading.

Fargo's own companions were somber as death. Cleon had climbed inside himself and hadn't said a word all morning.

Clementine Purdy stared at the swamp with fearful eyes. When she saw a large snake coiled on a log, she shuddered. When she saw an enormous alligator on a low hummock, she put her fist to her mouth. Once the gator was behind them she lowered her arm and said quietly, "I'm scared, Skye."

"About time," Fargo said, paddling.

"Really scared. I didn't realize—" Clementine stopped. "I could die."

"We all could."

Cleon broke his silence to say, "Never should have come."

Fargo spotted a big black bird soaring on outstretched wings high in the sky. He thought it might be a vulture.

"Both of you tried to warn me," Clementine said. "But a person never thinks it can happen to them."

"I do," Fargo said. He wondered if that helped keep him alive by keeping him sharp.

"Something else," Clementine said, and gestured at the

ghoulish landscape. "What sort of Indians live here? How do they survive?"

"How does anyone survive?" Fargo said. "They've learned to live off the land."

"What land?" Clementine said. "Except for a few spots here and there, it's muck and quicksand and water. Why would anyone live in a place like this when they could live anywhere else?"

Fargo shrugged. "Maybe they were driven here by stronger tribes. Maybe they liked it here."

"That's preposterous. No one in their right mind would like a swamp."

"Look at it their way," Fargo said. "It keeps them safe. No one else comes in this far. And those who do usually don't make it out again."

"They live here to keep their enemies away?" Clementine said dubiously.

The head of a snake rose out of the water not a yard from her side of the boat. She jerked back and opened her mouth to scream but didn't, and the head sank with hardly a ripple. "God help us," she breathed.

Clementine fell silent, wrapped her arms around herself, and closed her eyes.

It must have been an hour later that a bend hid the first boat and Cleon glanced over at Fargo and said, "I've made up my mind. You deserve to know."

"About?" Fargo said, not taking his gaze off the shadowy vegetation that grew uncomfortably near the side of the boat.

Cleon leaned toward him. "I like you and Miss Purdy. You've treated me decent."

"I'd have thrown you overboard long ago only she can't paddle worth a damn," Fargo joked.

Cleon didn't grin. "They're my pards. But it's wrong. And it will probably be soon so I'm tellin' you now."

"Get to the point."

Cleon glanced at the bend. "Bodean and Judson. They

plan to strand you and the others. They don't like that you whipped them. They don't like it all."

"They want everyone to suffer because of me?"

Their boat was almost to the bend, and Cleon answered quickly.

"They don't care about the others. They don't like outsiders. Especially those with the government."

In his wanderings Fargo had come across too much mindless hate. Hate that resulted in a lot of mindless killing.

Clementine's eyes were open. She had heard, and was paler than before.

"I don't know how they aim to go about it," Cleon said, "but I figured you should know."

"I'm obliged," Fargo said.

"We must inform Major Davenport right away," Clementine declared.

"It's best you keep it to yourself, ma'am," Cleon said. "They'll say it ain't so, and it'd be my word against theirs."

"He must be warned," Clementine insisted.

"You want me dead?" Cleon said. "Because Bodean and Judson will slit my throat as neat as you please for turnin' against my own kind."

The channel narrowed and Fargo had to push against the bank to keep from scraping. The bow cleared the curve, and ahead was a surprise; an acre or more of clear water and an island.

Major Davenport stood and pointed. "We'll camp there. I know it's early yet but the going is a lot harder than it was and the men are worn out."

They grounded their boats in a half-moon inlet and everyone climbed out. Two troopers were ordered to stand guard while the rest explored the island.

Major Davenport turned to proceed, and dug in his heels. "What have we here?"

It was a footpath. Not a game trail, but a path used by humans.

Fargo knelt to examine moccasin prints. "Some of these were made in the last day or so."

"The Kilatku," Davenport said. "We've found their village."

Fargo doubted it. The island wasn't big enough. He led the way inland, aware of rustlings that could be anything. When several sparrows took sudden wing, he nearly jumped. The swamp had him spooked, too.

The trail turned and turned again and came to an end at a clearing.

"What have we here?" Davenport said.

Five black circles marked where fires had been. Each was about ten feet from the other, and formed a giant ring.

Fargo squatted and poked at the charred bits. They were long cold and bore evidence of weathering. "These are old."

"How long ago?" Major Davenport asked.

"Months," Fargo said.

"If the Kilatku made them," Davenport said, "where have they been since?" Thoughtfully rubbing his chin, he turned to Morgan. "Sergeant, have the men build a fire and put coffee on. Then have them bring all our supplies from the boats." He surveyed the clearing and nodded. "This will make an excellent base of operations."

Fargo kept an eye on Bodean and Judson. They were standing apart and talking in hushed tones. They appeared to be arguing. He had an idea why when Bodean motioned at Clementine and Judson shook his head and said something that made Bodean glower with anger.

"Mr. Fargo," Major Davenport said, "while we're busying setting up, perhaps you would be so kind as to take our guides and explore the rest of this island?"

"I won't need all three," Fargo said. "Cleon can stay with you and help unload."

"Very well." Davenport smiled at Bodean and Judson. "Gentlemen, if you wouldn't mind. Assist Mr. Fargo."

Bodean scowled.

"We're happy to," Judson said, not sounding happy at all.

Cradling the Henry, Fargo crossed the clearing. Another trail led toward the opposite side of the island. "After you," he said.

"You're the scout," Bodean said. "You should go first."

Fargo shifted so the Henry's muzzle pointed at Bodean's belly. "I wasn't asking."

"What are you doin'?" Judson asked. "We're on the same side, remember?"

"Then you won't mind going ahead of me."

They looked at one another and Fargo caught a fleeting movement of Bodean's eyes.

"Sure, mister," Judson said. "Whatever you want." He moved in front of Bodean and they started off.

Fargo held back a few steps so they couldn't turn and jump him. He trained the Henry on the small of Bodean's back.

Vegetation enclosed them, worsening the gloom. Mosquitoes sought to cover every square inch of exposed skin. A green snake entwined around a branch slithered quickly away.

"God, I hate this," Judson said.

"We won't be here much longer," Bodean said.

Fargo was tempted to tell them he knew about their plan but they'd know how he found out and vent their wrath on Cleon.

Judson suddenly stopped.

Bodean happened to be looking down and walked into him, blurting, "What the hell?"

Crouching, Judson pointed at the undergrowth to the left and raised his rifle. "I saw someone."

"An Injun?" Bodean said, snapping his own rifle up.

"All I could see were eyes." Judson moved his head from side to side, searching. "They're gone now."

"You imagined it," Bodean said.

Fargo remembered his own experience. "Maybe not," he said.

"Do we go look?" Judson asked.

"Play right into their red hands, why don't you?" Bodean said. "They're probably waitin' to jump us."

Fargo couldn't see or hear anyone. "Keep moving," he directed.

"Like hell," Bodean said.

Jamming the Henry's muzzle into Bodean's back, Fargo said, "How about if I ask real nice?"

"Damn you," Bodean snarled. "The Kilatku are out there."

"Hope they are," Fargo said.

"Are you hankerin' to die?"

"If we make contact with them here," Fargo said, "we don't have to go any farther into the swamp."

"He's right," Judson said. "I'm all for that."

"They're liable to kill us and eat us, you damned simpletons," Bodean said.

Judson warily moved on. He went around a bend and then Bodean and finally Fargo—only to find that both swamp men had stopped.

"What the hell?" Bodean said.

Not ten feet away stood a boy. Small and thin-boned, he couldn't have seen more than ten winters. He wore a loincloth fashioned from a bear hide, and sandals, and nothing else. His hair was a disheveled mane, his face smeared with dirt. His arms were at his side and he appeared frozen except for his eyes, which blazed darkly.

"He must be a Kilatku," Judson said. He smiled and squatted and beckoned. "Come over here, boy. We won't hurt you."

"What do you think you're doin'?" Bodean asked.

"Hush. We make friends with him, the rest of his people will be friendly to us." Judson went on smiling and beckoning.

Fargo was watching the vegetation. The boy wouldn't be

alone. He was surprised when, showing no timidity whatsoever, the boy came toward them.

"See?" Judson beamed.

His face expressionless, the boy walked up to Judson. Still
showing no emotion, he whipped his arm up and plunged a
knife into Judson's eye.

12

Fargo didn't see the knife until the boy's arm moved. It was a sharpened flint with a bone handle.

Judson screamed and flung himself back against Bodean. In doing so, he tore the knife from the boy's grasp. He fell onto his shoulder with it jutting from his socket.

Bodean roared with fury and tried to bring his rifle to bear.

By then Fargo was next to him and swatted the barrel down. "Don't shoot!" he bellowed. Another bound, and he reached the boy just as the boy spun to run off. Lunging, he grabbed the boy's arm. The boy struck him, then tried to bite his fingers.

Worried that there might be more Kilatku about to attack, and wanting his hands free to use the Henry, Fargo clubbed the boy with the stock. Not with all his strength, but enough that the boy's eyes rolled up in his head and he crumbled.

Judson was shrieking and thrashing. Bodean tried to hold him still but Judson pushed him off, gripped the bone handle, and did the last thing he should have done—he wrenched on the knife. The flint blade came out—and so did his eye.

For a moment the tableau froze; Fargo, about to scoop up the boy; Bodean, shock on his face; Judson, gaping with his good eye at the eye he had just torn from its socket.

"Good God," Bodean said.

Letting out a bloodcurdling screech, Judson clutched at the ravaged socket and kicked and flung about in hysterics.

"Stop it," Bodean cried, attempting in vain to seize him.

Throwing the boy over his shoulder, Fargo said, "We have to get him back." He thought he glimpsed movement off in the riot of brown and green.

"I'm tryin'," Bodean fumed, and indeed he was, but each time he got hold of his friend, Judson pushed him away.

Boots pounded, and up rushed Major Davenport and Sergeant Morgan and a trooper. Davenport took in the situation at a glance and snapped commands. Instantly, Morgan and the soldier sprang to help Bodean. Between the three of them, with Morgan supplying most of the muscle, they subdued Judson.

Fargo covered the undergrowth. The boy didn't stir, and he worried that he'd struck him too hard.

Davenport came to his side. "The child did that?" he asked.

Fargo nodded.

The major stooped and picked up the blood-covered flint knife with the skewered eyeball. "This tribe is more primitive than I imagined."

More interested in preserving their hides, Fargo said, "We have to get the hell out of here."

"Certainly," Davenport said, and headed back, holding the knife as if it were a treasure.

Fargo came last. He glimpsed moving figures twice, or maybe it was the same one, shadowing them.

Clementine and Cleon and the other troopers were anxiously waiting with their weapons ready.

"Look at this," Davenport declared, waving the knife. "We've established contact."

Morgan and Bodean deposited Judson by the fire. Thankfully, Judson had passed out.

Fargo carefully placed the boy on his back.

"The poor child," Clementine said, falling to her knees next to him.

"He's the one who stabbed Judson," Fargo enlightened her.

"But he's so young," Clementine said, placing a hand on

the boy's cheek. "So innocent. You must have scared him and he reacted without thinking."

"He was waiting for us."

"All by himself?" Clementine gazed about the clearing. "Where are the rest of his people? Where are the warriors?"

Fargo was wondering the same thing. It made no sense for the Kilatku to have the boy confront them by his lonesome.

Clementine gently shook the child's shoulder. "I'll bring him around."

"No need," Bodean said, stepping over and drawing his knife. "I'm fixin' to gut the little bastard."

"You'll do no such thing," Clementine said.

"Watch me, bitch." Bodean bent and reached to grab the boy's long hair.

"No!" Clementine cried, flinging out an arm.

Bodean cuffed her.

"Stop him!" Major Davenport shouted.

Fargo was already in motion. He rammed the Henry's barrel into Bodean's belly, and when Bodean doubled over, swept the rifle up and around. At the *thunk* Bodean dropped like a poled ox.

"Thank you," Clementine said breathlessly.

Fargo stepped back. Cleon and Morgan were tending to Judson. The major was engrossed in the knife. The troopers were waiting for orders. No one paid any attention to the vegetation. It was up to him to make a quick circuit, seeking sign of the Kilatku. There was none. He suspected they had gone to ground and would wait for a chance to rescue the boy.

Davenport approached, still enrapt by the knife. "If this is the best they can arm themselves, we don't have a thing to worry about."

"There are bound to be more of them," Fargo said.

"The trinkets we brought will win them over," Davenport predicted. "I'm surprised the surveyor didn't have them eating out of his hand."

"You're putting the cart before the horse."

"Because I haven't met them yet?" Davenport wagged the flint knife and laughed.

Cleon turned and glared. "What's so funny, mister, with my friend lyin' over here half blinded for the rest of his days?"

No one had been paying attention to the one responsible— Fargo was still watching the vegetation—so when the boy suddenly shot to his feet and bounded for the brush, no one was near enough to grab him except Clementine, but all she did was cry out, "Hey there! Stop!"

Without breaking stride the boy plunged into the dark growth.

Fargo ran to the edge of the clearing. It would be foolhardy to go in there not knowing how many Kilatku were lying in wait.

Davenport and a trooper joined him. "Let him go," the major said. "We don't need him and I don't intend to punish him over what he did to Judson. I don't wage war on children."

"Little gnits grow to be gnats, sir," the trooper said.

"That will be enough of that kind of talk," Davenport snapped.

For once Fargo was in agreement with the major. Some whites felt that the solution to the Indian "problem," as they called it, was to kill every last Indian—men, women and children.

"I'm sorry," Clementine said, coming over. "It happened so fast."

"That's all right, my dear," Davenport said. "Look at the bright side." He beamed and gestured at the trooper and they walked off.

"Bright side?" Clementine asked.

"There's an idiot born every minute," Fargo said.

"Poor Judson. Sergeant Morgan says he might not live. That the next twenty-four hours will tell."

"Morgan has seen a lot of wounds." Fargo recollected the sergeant saying at one time or another he'd tangled with the Comanches, the Dakotas and the Blackfeet.

"I still can't believe that little boy did something so horrible," Clementine said. "Someone must have put him up to it."

"Or he hates us."

"What did we ever do to him?"

"We're white."

"Not everyone hates on account of skin color," Clementine said. "I don't."

"He's not you."

"Yes, but we're all human beings."

Fargo grunted. She was one of *those*. People who took it for granted the whole world thought the same as they did.

"You do that a lot," Clementine remarked.

Fargo turned, and stopped. It had suddenly occurred to him that everyone was at the clearing; no one was guarding the boats. Hurrying to the path to the inlet, he broke into a jog. When he reached it he breathed a sigh of relief.

The boats hadn't been taken or cast adrift.

Climbing into one, Fargo sat and placed the Henry across his legs. At least in the boat he was somewhat safe from snakes and gators.

As if to remind him they were out there, an alligator swam past twenty yards out.

To the north, a snake was hanging from a tree, evidently waiting for prey to pounce on.

Fargo told himself that from here on out, he'd fight shy of swamps. They had a thousand and one ways to kill a man, and none of them pleasant.

A twig crunched, and down the path came Clementine Purdy, looking for all the world as if she were taking a Sunday stroll. "There you are. You ran off without saying a word."

Fargo patted the boat. "Without these, none of us might make it back."

"Ah." Clementine stood near the bow and folded her arms. "I'm afraid I'd be helpless without you and the major."

"Helpless as hell," Fargo said.

Clementine's lips pinched tight. "There's no need to be insulting."

"You shouldn't be here."

"We've been all through that. More than once. I have my duty. A greater cause, if you will."

"Dying so someone can make a map doesn't strike me as much of a cause."

"I have the distinct impression that you don't think very highly of me."

"I think highly of your body."

Clementine blinked. "How can you, at a time like this? With Judson lying back there at death's door?"

Fargo was about to say that Judson planned to strand them and got what he deserved, when he spied movement in the vegetation. "Hold it," he said, and went to raise his rifle.

"What is it?" Clementine asked, swiveling in the direction he was looking.

The next moment a figure hurtled from concealment with a knife in one hand and a club in the other, and sprang at her.

13

Fargo had the Henry up and pointed, and for a split instant, he hesitated.

It was a woman, not a warrior. Small, slightly built, naked from the waist up, wearing a short bear-hide skirt of sorts, split for ease of movement. Her face was twisted in fury as she let out a fierce cry and raised her club to bash Clementine Purdy over the head.

Fargo shot the club. The woman was so close he couldn't miss, but he was gambling with Clementine's life.

The slug smashed the club from the woman's grasp and wrenched her arm. Yelping in pain, she stopped in her tracks but only for a second. She started at Clementine again and raised her knife.

In a bound Fargo was out of the boat. He smashed the barrel against the woman's forearm and she yelped and the knife went flying. Sticking his foot out, he tripped her and she pitched to her knees. He pointed the Henry's muzzle at her face and said gruffly, "That's enough."

She might not savvy his words but she understood the tone. Holding her wrist, she glared at him and at Clementine and said something in her tongue.

"Don't shoot her," Clementine said.

Fargo wasn't about to. But someone else thought he was. Out of the growth raced the small boy. He ran to the woman and threw his arms around her neck. Fear lit his eyes, and he stood between her and the Henry, shielding her with his body.

"Her son?" Clementine guessed.

Fargo lowered the rifle, but not all the way. Moving around the pair, he kicked the flint knife and the club out of their reach.

"Why did she attack us?" Clementine asked.

"How the hell would I know?" Fargo scanned the swamp growth for more Kilatku but the woman and boy appeared to be alone.

"You could try to be nicer to people," Clementine said. She stepped nearer to the pair, smiled, and squatted. "How do you do?" she said. "Do either of you speak English?"

They stared.

"Let me," Fargo said, suspecting it would be useless. He tried anyway; he told them he was not their enemy in Spanish, in the Sioux tongue, in Apache, in the Blackfoot language. He might as well be speaking Martian.

The woman kept looking from him to Clementine and back again. She was a frightened doe poised to bolt.

"Look at her," Clementine said. "Does she look in good shape to you?"

No, Fargo reflected, she didn't. The woman was as dirty as the boy and scratched from briars and limbs. Both had their ribs showing.

"I wonder when they ate last." Clementine smiled and slowly reached toward the woman, saying, "Don't be afraid. I want to be your friend."

The woman did an incredible thing. She screeched in mortal terror and flung herself and her son back onto the ground.

"What in the world?" Clementine blurted.

Clasping the boy tight, the woman babbled and shook her head, her eyes riveted to the tips of Clementine's fingers.

"What do you make of it?"

Fargo was going to say, "How the hell should I know?" again, but said simply, "Beats me." He bent and held out his hand to help the woman to sit up, and damned if she didn't screech louder and skittle backward on her shoulders and hips. She stopped when he pulled his hand back.

"Strange," Clementine said. "It's as if she's afraid of being touched."

A vague recollection pricked at Fargo's memory but he couldn't give it form and substance.

Boots scuffed the ground, and Major Davenport and two troopers arrived. "What's going on here?" the officer demanded, and saw the mother and her boy. "By God, two of them."

Continuing to hold her son as if in fear for his life, the woman sat up.

"She attacked me but Skye stopped her," Clementine said.

"So their women are as hostile as their men," Davenport said.

"What men?" Fargo said.

"Eh?"

"We haven't come across a single warrior yet," Fargo pointed out.

"They're out there," Davenport said. "They have to be."

"Then why haven't they attacked?"

Davenport scratched his chin. "I confess I'm mystified. But it's a golden opportunity. We'll take this pair to camp and hold them until their people reveal themselves."

"Is that wise?" Clementine asked.

"Unless we want them harassing us from now until doomsday, it is," Davenport said. "We won't harm them. That will show the other Kilatku we're friendly." He gestured at a trooper. "Private Lyle, help them to their feet."

"I wouldn't," Clementine said.

Private Lyle slung his rifle and stepped closer and held out his hand.

Jumping up, the woman and the boy cried out and frantically retreated until they bumped against a boat. Halting, they held one another and quaked.

"Why, they're scared to death," Davenport said.

"Of what?" Clementine said.

"Isn't it obvious? They don't want to be taken prisoner. Not that they have any choice." Davenport nodded at the other trooper. "Assist Private Lyle. Don't lay a hand on them but keep them between you and if they try to run, stop them."

"Yes, sir."

Fargo went along to the clearing. He was still concerned about the boats but he was more worried that something would happen to the mother and boy and bring the wrath of the whole tribe down on their heads.

A bandage had been applied to Judson's eye. He was unconscious, Cleon watching over him.

Bodean had recovered, and the moment Fargo appeared, Bodean strode toward him. He didn't even glance at the mother and the boy.

Fargo thumbed back the Henry's hammer.

"Twice now you've beat on me, you son of a bitch," Bodean growled. "There won't be a third time."

"I couldn't let you kill him," Fargo said.

"He put out Judson's eye," Bodean snarled. "Judson might die."

"I'm sorry for him—" Fargo lied.

"Like hell you are. You haven't cottoned to us from the start. That fight in the saloon, and now this. I'm tellin' you. If Judson gives up the ghost, that boy is dead. You hear me?"

"It's up to Davenport to—" Fargo again tried to get a few words in.

"He can go to hell too, him and that female, both, with their crazy notion of makin' friends with the Kilatku." Bodean swore. "That boy showed us how they feel about us. It's their hides or ours, and I don't intend to stop breathin'."

"You try to hurt him, I'll stop you."

"Next time I won't give you the chance." Wheeling, Bodean stormed off.

Mother and son were by the fire, flanked by troopers, whispering.

Fargo went over. He could use a gallon of whiskey but coffee would have to do. As he was taking his first sip he acquired an unwanted shadow.

"I need you to scout the island," Major Davenport said.

"And when the Kilatku jump me, where will you be?"

"The general forced me to bring you along," Davenport said. "He claimed you're the best tracker alive, and the best Indian fighter, besides. Well, here's your chance to prove it."

"Why not let them come to us?"

"Is the great scout afraid?" Davenport taunted.

"The great scout isn't stupid," Fargo said.

"Something is fishy about all this," Davenport said. "We need to know if they're out there or if the woman and the boy attacked us on their own."

Sergeant Morgan had come over and was listening. "I'll go with him, sir," he volunteered.

"I need you here," Davenport said. "I can't afford to lose you."

"But you can afford to lose me?" Fargo said.

"Yes. You haven't impressed me much so far. Here's your chance."

Fargo was about to tell the bastard that he didn't give a damn what Davenport thought of him when he noticed Clementine wringing her hands and biting her lip.

"Hell," he said.

"You'll do it?"

Instead of answering, Fargo turned and was in the insect-and-reptile infested vegetation before he could come to his senses. He went a few yards and crouched. A mosquito buzzed his ear but he didn't swat it. He stayed motionless, braced for a war whoop and the rush of painted forms.

No one appeared.

The flies went on buzzing and crickets went on chirping. Frogs croaked and a brown snake crawled lazily along.

Fargo not only had to watch out for the Kilatku, he had to be careful where he stepped and make sure the plants he brushed against didn't harbor venomous death. It was nerve-racking, worse than being on a scout in Apache country. He covered barely ten yards in ten minutes.

He might have gone on at his snail's pace but sharp cries broke out at the clearing, and Major Davenport bellowed, "Stop her, someone! Don't let them get away!"

Behind Fargo the undergrowth crackled, and through it came the woman and her son. They were small and thin but fleet as deer and would pass within a stone's toss of where Fargo was hunkered. Waiting until they were almost abreast of him, he darted over. His foot snagged in a vine and he tripped. He didn't fall, but it slowed him enough that the woman and her offspring bounded past.

Fargo gave chase. Try as he might, he couldn't gain. Sweat streaming from every pore, he avoided a coiled snake and a large spider that dangled in his path.

His instincts told him they were near the end of the island. Sure enough, he burst into the open at the water's edge and lurched to a stop. He spotted the woman and the boy to his right.

The next heartbeat the water bubbled and roiled and out of its dark depths rose a gator.

14

Fargo's first thought was that it was one of the giant ones and it would attack him as the other gator had done to the hapless trooper. But it wasn't a third the size, and as fast as it had surfaced, the alligator submerged again.

Fargo went after the woman and the boy. They were hugging the shore and repeatedly glanced back. He was startled when they unexpectedly veered into the water and seemed to run across it. When he got to the spot he saw that a submerged spine of land ran from the island toward a distant hummock. Only a few inches of water covered it.

He shouldn't be surprised that the Kilatku knew ways of navigating the swamp no one else did. They'd lived here for hundreds of years, and could travel with ease where others struggled and floundered.

He stuck after them. It could be they'd been the only ones on the island. The rest of the tribe might not know about him and the others. The mother would spread the alarm, and the next thing, a war party would be sent to exterminate the invaders.

Fargo couldn't let that happen. He needed to overtake the pair but instead lost ground. The submerged spine wasn't much wider than his boots and he had to go slower than he wanted.

The woman and her child reached the hummock and stopped to look back. The woman showed no fear. Why should she? She was in her element.

It surprised him that she didn't keep fleeing. She waited until he was fifty or sixty feet out, then turned and resumed her flight. It enabled him to cut the distance by half.

Beyond the far side of the hummock was more odious swamp. A bog gurgled and burped and gave off reeking fumes.

For the next half an hour Fargo scrambled and waded through and over some of the most hellish terrain he'd ever come across. Twice he almost stepped on cottonmouths. He was passing a thick growth of reeds when he saw a huge snout and glaring eyes; he was fortunate the alligator didn't pounce.

Mosquitoes were legion. Other insects he didn't know the names of swooped at him. A dragonfly the size of a bird circled his head a few times before streaking off.

The woman and the boy crossed a downed cypress. When he reached it, he clambered up, only to find his wet boots and the slick bark made for a slippery combination. Halfway across, he looked down to find quicksand.

Fargo froze. He had been in quicksand before and gotten out. But something told him that if he fell, he'd be sucked under so rapidly, escape would be impossible.

Carefully sliding first one foot and then the other, he inched into the clear.

When he reached the end of the log, he let out a long breath he hadn't realized he was holding.

Up ahead, the woman and the boy had once again stopped and were waiting.

"What the hell?" Fargo said. She *wanted* him to keep following her. She was luring him deeper in so Kilatku warriors could finish him.

For a few moments Fargo considered going back. But no. He had come this far. He would see it through. If she did lead him into an ambush, he'd go down fighting.

When he began moving, so did she.

Fargo lost track of time. He lost track of the miles.

He followed secret paths that no white foot had ever trod,

or so he thought until he came to a stretch of dry mud and beheld an old boot print.

Fargo stopped. He spied others, evidence that several whites had passed this way. The surveyors, he reckoned, and noticed that there were no tracks pointing the other way. They had gone in—and not come out again.

Land appeared. Real, honest-to-God dry land. If it was an island it was many times larger than any other.

There were trees and wildflowers and warbling birds, a patch of paradise in the depths of hell.

The woman reached the shore and once more she and her boy stopped.

This time they stayed put.

Fargo finally set foot on solid ground. He looked at her and she looked at him. He couldn't figure out what she was up to. He didn't point the rifle. He simply waited to see what she would do.

He wondered why she wasn't afraid of him. Was it because he'd stopped Bodean from killing her son?

She said a few words in her own tongue.

Fargo shook his head and said, "Sorry, lady, but I don't savvy."

Turning, she beckoned, and headed inland along a well-worn footpath.

He sensed her village was near.

Soon the trees gave way to twenty to thirty acres of cleared land, and over forty lodges. Constructed of reeds and stripped branches, they were conical in shape with a small opening for entering and leaving and an air hole at the top.

Fargo stopped in midstride and his blood chilled in his veins. "God Almighty," he blurted.

Bodies littered the ground. Men, women, children, infants. They had been dead a long while. Most were piles of shriveled skin and pale bones.

Strangely, few scavengers had been at them. Even the vultures had left them alone.

A great sadness came over the woman and the boy.

Her eyes filled with tears, and she gestured and spoke at length. She was trying to tell him something, something important, he suspected.

Fargo looked, trying to figure it out. He moved among the dead. Their bared teeth, their fingers clawing at the sky; these people had died grisly deaths, in great torment. He wondered why they had been left to rot.

He came to a dead woman and bent, but not too close. Her face was as sunken and shriveled as the rest but she had more skin than most. Skin marked by dark blotches, some of which had dry scabs.

Disease, Fargo realized with a jolt. The entire village had been wiped out by sickness. He remembered the same thing had happened to the Mandans and several other tribes, and a terrible suspicion took hold.

At the very center of the village was an open space, and there, placed in a row, were dead white men. All had been horribly mutilated and finished off by having their throats slit.

Fargo had found the surveyor and five of the six men in his party. Vultures and other scavengers had been at them and there wasn't much left.

Fargo pondered, trying to reconstruct the sequence of events. The Kilatku had brought the surveyor and his men to their village. That much was obvious. But as friends or as enemies?

Just beyond stood a giant clay pot next to a fire pit. On an impulse, Fargo went over and looked in. His stomach churned and he swallowed bitter bile.

It was a cooking pot. Inside lay bones that had been gnawed clean of the meat. He could see the teeth marks. A skull leered at him, and by its size, Fargo had a hunch this was the sixth member of the surveying team.

So the Kilatku *were* cannibals. They'd captured the white intruders and boiled and ate one of their victims.

Was that what made them sick? Was that how they came down with the disease?

Like the Mandans and other tribes before them, the Kilatku had no immunity to white disease. It must have spread like wildfire. Too late, they'd realized the whites were to blame, and massacred the others. And then what? Waited around to die? Or fled into the depths of the Archaletta Swamp?

Fargo turned and almost collided with the woman and her son. She had a strange expression on her face. "I'm sorry," he said. Cannibals or not, the Kilatku didn't deserve this.

She gazed at the bodies and bowed her head and a tear trickled down her cheek.

"Are there any more of you?" Fargo asked, knowing full well it was useless.

She looked at him quizzically.

Fargo pointed at several dead Kilatku and then at her and the boy and arched his eyebrows and gestured at the surrounding island and the swamp.

A gleam came into her eyes. She opened her mouth and said what sounded for all the world like, "Ah." The lines of sorrow on her face deepened. She said a few words and touched her chest and the boy's.

Fargo thought he understood. She and her son were the last of their kind. "Damn."

A log had been placed not far from the pot. He walked over and sat. He was suddenly tired. The ordeal of following her through the swamp had caught up with him. He set the Henry's stock on the ground and leaned his forehead against the barrel.

The woman and the boy sat next to him. She showed no fear. She touched her bosom again and the boy's chest and pointed at his own. She did that several times while giving him a questioning look.

"You don't mean—?" Fargo said, and realized she did. She was offering herself to him, offering to be his woman and the boy to be his son.

Fargo was about to give an emphatic shake of his head but changed his mind. He would do what he could for her, short of *that*. But what could he do, other than take her back to civilization?

He wondered how it was that she and the boy hadn't come down with the disease. They must be immune, probably the only ones in the tribe.

She smiled, and to his consternation he saw that her teeth had been filed to points.

Fargo needed to rest. He pantomimed stretching and yawning and got up. Since he wasn't about to sleep in a village of the dead, he walked to the outskirts and selected a grassy spot.

Clouds continued to scuttle across the sky like so many great gray crabs.

The woman and the boy had followed him. She sat cross-legged and said something.

Fargo shook his head and propped his hands behind him.

He reckoned to nap for a bit and head back. With a little luck he could rejoin the others before sunset.

Again the woman addressed him and pointed at the woods. She seemed agitated.

Fargo didn't see any cause for alarm. All the warriors were dead. They weren't near water so gators weren't a worry. Nor had he seen any of the big snakes.

This was about as safe a spot as any.

The woman extended her finger at the village, her agitation worse.

Again Fargo thought he understood. "I doubt I'll catch whatever it was." Closing his eyes, he drifted off.

When he opened them again, night had fallen.

15

"Hell," Fargo said, and sat up. He jammed his hat on, grabbed the Henry, and gave a start. The woman and the boy were gone. He'd taken it for granted they would be there when he woke up.

Fargo stood. A breeze had picked up, a warm wind that did nothing to relieve the heat and the humidity.

With the fall of darkness, the swamp had come alive. From out of it rose the roars and grunts of gators, the thrum of a thousand bullfrogs, the occasional shrieks of quarry.

Cradling the Henry, Fargo moved toward the village. If the woman was anywhere, he figured, she was there.

The cone lodges reared like oversized beehives. The bodies were hard to make out.

Fargo stopped and hollered, "Woman, where the hell are you?" She wouldn't understand but she would know he was up and return.

From the woods came crackling and rustling noises.

Fargo spun. It must be an animal. When nothing appeared he debated what to do. The bodies lying everywhere gnawed at his nerves. It didn't help that although the victims had been there a spell, the smell of death was in the air.

Fargo decided to look for her. He skirted several still forms. He was passing a hut when he detected movement inside. Moving to the opening, he dropped to a knee. "Is that you?"

No one answered.

Fargo bent and looked in. It was black as pitch. No way in hell was he going in there.

Increasingly uneasy, he prowled the village from end to end. He found no trace of the woman or the boy. He was alone with the Reaper's handiwork.

Since he wasn't about to try to return to Clementine and the others in the dark without the woman to guide him, he ventured into the woods and gathered downed limbs.

Presently, he had a small fire crackling near where he'd slept.

In all that vastness, his was the only light.

Fargo thought of Clementine and her willowy thighs. "Hell," he grumbled.

There was still no sign of the Kilatku woman and her son.

An hour became two and Fargo regretted taking his nap. He was too awake to fall back to sleep.

He wished he had the Ovaro. He wished they were in the Rockies or on the plains. Anywhere but here.

"Listen to me," Fargo said in disgust. "Whining to myself."

He added a branch to the fire and sat back. Tilting his head, he looked for a glimpse of the stars, in vain.

An owl hooted. Another bull alligator let the swamp know it was in a mating mood.

Fargo gazed at the cone huts, wondering if there was anything in them worth taking back. As poor as the Kilatku were, he doubted it.

He yawned and stretched and listened to the crickets and the frogs.

A new sound registered, faintly at first, a *scrape-scrape-scrape* as of something being dragged. It came from the village.

Puzzled, Fargo set the Henry across his legs. He tried to assign the noise to a cause and couldn't.

A shape appeared. Small and spindly, it moved in short jerks. And it was coming in his direction.

Fargo stood. He saw other shapes, four, five, six, all moving stiffly as if something was wrong with their limbs.

"What in the hell?"

From out of the night to his right flashed the woman and the boy. She cried out and gripped his hand and pulled.

Fargo stood firm. She wanted him to get out of there but he'd be damned if he'd run. The strange shapes had to come into the firelight to reach him, and he could drop them with the Henry.

The woman glanced at the figures and uttered another cry. She stopped pulling, seized her son, and fled.

"Big help you were," Fargo said. He was so intent on the stiff figures that he didn't think to add more fuel to the fire.

A sudden gust of wind reduced the flames to tiny fingers. It reduced the circle of light, too.

Fargo grabbed for a piece of firewood just as another gust caused the flames to flicker and shrink and go out entirely.

Bending, Fargo puffed on the embers. He expected the fire to flare to renewed life but it didn't. He was shrouded in gloom so black, his hand was invisible at arm's length.

He looked up. The shapes were moving faster. On two legs, which told him he was wrong about the disease wiping out everyone except the woman and the boy. Other Kilatku had survived. He raised the Henry and tried to fix a bead on a lurching silhouette.

A hand fell on his shoulder.

Thinking it was the woman, Fargo turned. The face nearly touching his wasn't hers. It was a warrior's, the skin blotched, the flesh diseased, the lips curled from filed teeth, the eyes seeming to glow with sheer savagery. The man stank to high heaven.

"Jesus," Fargo said.

The warrior bit at his neck. Fargo flung himself back. He tripped and sprawled and the apparition came after him. Slamming his boot into the Kilatku's chest, he sent the reeking ruin stumbling.

Shuffling sounds came from all sides. The others were closing in.

Heaving upright, Fargo pointed the Henry at the warrior who had tried to bite him. The man lurched and he fired point-blank into the scrawny chest. Whirling, he shot a Kilatku reaching for him with fingers hooked like talons.

He backpedaled, collided with another, and butt-stroked the man's head.

Yet another darted in fast and low, arms spread, mouth agape and showing those awful teeth.

Fargo shot him. Then he did as the woman had done: he ran. Should one of the warriors bite him, he might come down with the disease. He wouldn't risk that.

He was lucky they hadn't used weapons. Maybe in their ravaged state they weren't thinking straight.

No sooner did that cross his mind than a Kilatku was in front of him and a flint knife slashed. He sidestepped, felt a sting and rammed his Henry into the blotched face. The Kilatku went down and he leaped over him and was in the woods.

Fargo didn't stop. He needed to put distance between him and the village. He looked for the woman but didn't see her.

The woods seemed otherworldly. The moss-covered trees were misshapen and drooped, the undergrowth was a sickly hue. Not a single animal cry broke the stillness.

For one of the few times in his life, Fargo lost all sense of direction. Without the stars, he couldn't tell north from south or east from west. He was truly and literally lost.

The trees ended at water. He was in it up to his ankles before he stopped. Retreating onto dry land, he hunkered next to a cypress.

All he could do now was wait and see if the warriors came after him.

He was panting, and slowed his breathing. He must stay perfectly still and be completely quiet. He was the hunted, not the hunter.

An hour went by. Two.

Once, he thought he heard shuffling. Another time, there was a shout, a man's voice. No one answered.

Toward dawn he started to doze. Jerking his head up, he shook himself to stay awake.

Gradually, the sky brightened from black to gray. The forest acquired colors and depth.

Fargo looked at the water, expecting swamp, and smiled in surprise. He'd stumbled on a spring. Going over, he lay flat. The water appeared to be safe to drink. He dipped a hand in and took a wary sip. It tasted as water should. As thirsty as he was, he drank in great gulps but had the presence of mind not to drink too much. Taking off his hat, he lowered his face. The coolness revitalized him. He raised his head and shook it and drops flew.

Fargo sat up and reached for his hat and his hand came down on something that writhed and hissed. Recoiling, he jumped up and caught sight of a snake moving away.

"Damn this swamp."

Jamming his hat on, Fargo reclaimed the Henry. He wasn't sticking around. The Kilatku would be searching for him, and they knew the swamp better than he did.

In a quarter of a mile he reached the shore. Paralleling it, he sought sign of the secret trail that brought him there, the route the woman had used. For once his knack for landmarks failed him. One area of swamp looked the same as every other.

He hiked around a headland and there they were: the woman and the boy, crouched, apparently waiting.

She stood and smiled.

"I'm right pleased to see you again, too," Fargo confessed. It felt peculiar, him having to rely on someone else to get around.

Reaching out, she took his free hand and placed it on her left breast.

"What the hell?"

She bobbed her small chin at his groin and her smile widened.

"Damn, woman. You can't mean what I think you mean," Fargo said in amazement.

She squeezed his fingers so his fingers squeezed her breast.

"You do mean it."

The woman rimmed her lips with her tongue.

Fargo looked at her pointed teeth and at the boy and off toward the village and thought of the cooking pot. "I couldn't even if I wanted to."

She pinched her nipple with his fingertips.

"Enough." Fargo pulled his hand away. "I can't believe I'm saying this, but no thanks."

The woman frowned.

Fargo gestured at the swamp. "We have to get out of here. Will you lead me back to the others?"

She stared at his crotch.

Just then, off in the woods, a scream rose to the clouds. It was a human cry, a man on the verge of oblivion or in the throes of madness, or maybe both. It sank and rose again to a keening pitch of despair.

"Hell," Fargo said, and motioned again at the foreboding swamp.

The woman appeared scared. Grasping her son's hand, she finally did as he wanted.

"Here we go again," Fargo said.

16

By the middle of the morning he'd made up his mind that he was never setting foot in a swamp again.

The woman led him by a different route. A harder route, with more bogs and quicksand to avoid, and stretches where he was up to his waist in water. She constantly looked back as if she feared they were pursued.

Snakes and gators were as common as mosquitoes. Despite the clouds, the heat climbed and the humidity drenched him as much as the water.

It got so it ate at Fargo's nerves. He jumped at splashes. He was irritated as hell at the perpetual swarms of bugs.

Swamps—some swamps, anyway, and this one in particular—were living hells he could do without.

The woman stopped on a low spine of dry land to rest. Her son curled up with his head in her lap and was immediately asleep.

Fargo couldn't sleep if he tried. He was too on edge.

Taking a seat, he wriggled his wet toes. He'd need a new pair of boots when this was over. Provided he lived.

The woman was staring at him. She smiled her pointed-teeth smile and reached out for his hand and placed it on her breast.

"Oh, hell," Fargo said. "Is that all you think about?" He wondered if there was some meaning to it that eluded him.

She squeezed his fingers and looked at him hopefully.

Fargo shook his head and pulled his hand back. "Quit doing that."

Crestfallen, the woman averted her face.

Fargo let out a sigh. "When I get back to civilization," he promised himself aloud, "I'm going to find a willing filly and spend a week in bed." Maybe longer.

Sudden splashing to the south made him stiffen. Probably a gator, or a fish. He relaxed and plucked at a stem of grass and stuck it between his teeth. It tasted bitter and he spit it out.

More splashing brought him to his feet. It was louder and closer. Something was out there, something big.

The woman eased her son's head off her leg and rose. She, too, appeared worried.

"What now?"

The splashing continued and a great bulk lumbered into view.

"Goddamn swamps," Fargo said.

It was a bear, one of the largest black bears he'd ever set eyes on. Snuffling and casting about for food, it hadn't noticed them yet.

Fargo raised the Henry but he would rather not use it. It was a fine man-stopper but not so fine at bringing down buffs or bears.

The woman bent and snatched her sleeping son into her arms. She whispered and began to back away.

Fargo thought it wiser not to move until the bear had gone by. But he backed after her, covering the black bear and praying it didn't look in their direction.

The bear huffed and lunged, dipping its head in the water. When it rose up, a fish was clamped between its teeth. It bit, gulped and the fish was gone.

Fargo imagined those iron jaws closing on him.

The woman reached the end of the rise and stopped. She acted uncertain whether to go or stay put.

The black bear was forty feet out, head low to the water.

Fargo began to think it would pass them by. A mass of muscle and fat that huge would be next to impossible to stop.

Uttering a cry, the boy woke up and looked around in confusion.

The bear stopped. Its head swiveled and it saw them, and sniffed.

Fargo smothered an impulse to swear. It was a good thing he wasn't playing poker. His luck of late was downright pitiful.

The woman was on the move, the boy at her side. She whispered, her eyes white with fright.

Retreating, Fargo watched the bear. It sniffed some more and waded toward them, raising a wake. A frog swam madly from its path.

Fargo was in water up to his ankles. The woman had found another of those partially submerged ridges. He needed to watch where he stepped so he didn't slip but he didn't dare take his eyes off the damn bear.

With a final splash the beast reached the rise. It shook itself and moved to where they had been sitting and sniffed.

On Fargo's right a gator surfaced. Not one of the giants but big enough that it could drag him under. It eyed them as if it were sizing them up to do just that.

The woman moved faster. Fargo tried to keep up but the footing was treacherous. He glanced down and when he looked up again, the black bear was on the near end of the rise and entering the water.

"Son of a bitch."

At the same time, the alligator flicked its long tail and glided slowly toward them.

"Eat this," Fargo said, and spinning, he aimed between the alligator's eyes and fired. The gator reared and went into a series of violent rolls, over and over and over. When it stopped it was belly-up.

Fargo thought that the sound of the shot might spook the bear into running off. He should have known better.

It was still coming, and coming faster.

His next step back brought him to a small patch of dry ground. This was where he would make his stand. He centered the rifle's sights on the bear's broad chest. The skull was too thick; the slug would likely glance off.

The bear plowed through the water, raising spray in all directions. It came abreast of the dead alligator and veered. Sniffing noisily, it nosed the gator's belly. Its maw opened, blood and guts spewed, and the bear half lifted the gator and turned around and lumbered off with its prize.

"I'll be damned," Fargo said.

They pressed on.

To his delight the clouds began to thin, and it wasn't long before the sun broke through.

The temperature climbed another ten degrees.

Fargo daydreamed of the miles-high Rockies with their peaks mantled in snow. He would give anything to be there now. He'd strip naked and jump into a high-country lake fed by runoff and let the cold into his marrow.

Along about two in the afternoon the woman stopped and pointed and said a few words.

Fargo could have hugged her. It was the island, at last. They'd come up on it from the east. He didn't see smoke or hear voices, which bothered him. He found out why when they reached the clearing.

No one was there. The packs were gone.

Cold embers showed that the fire had long since gone out.

A host of flies buzzed around a body that lay belly-down across the way. It was Private Lyle; he'd been stabbed, not once, but several times.

When Fargo rolled the body over, a small snake shot past his boot.

A sinking feeling in his gut, Fargo raced down the trail to the boats. Halfway he came on the body of another trooper. This one had been shot.

Dread gripped him. If all the boats were gone he was stranded in the heart of the Archaletta.

At the last bend he stopped to listen. He heard the lapping of water, nothing more.

The boats weren't there. Davenport and the rest had abandoned him.

Fargo tried to tell himself that Clementine wouldn't do that, but how well did he really know her? To keep from thinking about it, he read the sign.

There were so many footprints, it was difficult.

Deep heel marks suggested that two men shoved the first boat off and climbed in. The two weren't wearing army issue boots, so it had to be Bodean and Cleon or Bodean and Judson.

Major Davenport and Sergeant Morgan had shoved off a second boat, Clementine and probably Cleon a third.

That left one boat unaccounted for.

Fargo scanned the swamp, not really expecting to find it. But he did. It had floated a good seventy feet and was lodged against a log.

"Thank you, God," Fargo said. He went to wade out but the woman grabbed his wrist. By her pantomime, she was saying she didn't want to go.

Fargo went anyway, and she sulkily followed. He swung around a deep pool, edged along a bog and reached the log. The woman stopped but he clambered onto it and reached the boat. The paddles were in the bottom, and a pack was in the bow.

Settling himself, he braced a paddle against the log to free the boat and stroked over to the woman. He motioned for her to climb in but she just stood there.

Fargo was eager to get under way. The others might not be far ahead. Perhaps he could overtake them before nightfall. He held out his hand and the woman took it. He had to tug twice before she nervously placed her foot in the boat. Then she balked. He tugged some more but she refused to climb in.

"It's only a damn boat." Fargo was tempted to haul her off her feet but she might bolt. Inspiration struck, and he placed his hand on her tit and squeezed.

The woman lit up like a candle.

"Get your ass in here and I'll pinch the nipple too," Fargo said.

She eased her other leg in, helped her son, and they sat behind him.

"If that's all it takes to win an argument with a female," Fargo remarked, "I'll be squeezing tits from now until doomsday."

She smiled that hideous smile.

"The pinching will have to wait," Fargo said, and brought the bow around. It felt great to have a boat under him. No more worrying about snakes and less worry about gators. He almost whooped for joy.

He made good progress for half a mile or more and then he lost his way. He had to backtrack twice. Finally he found the channel he wanted and paddled twice as hard.

When the woman plucked at his whangs he paid her no mind. He wasn't slowing for any reason. She plucked again and he glanced at her and she pointed.

They were passing cypress trees. In the shadows bobbed another of their boats.

"What the hell?"

It took some doing to bring their own around. As he approached he saw a limp hand sticking over the side.

Fargo drifted the final few yards, his hand on his Colt.

The last trooper lay on his belly, his leg bent unnaturally under him. A pool of blood glistened in the sunlight.

"Hell," Fargo said. He leaned out to grab the other boat, and the head and neck of a water moccasin rose above the gunwale.

17

Fargo snatched his hand away just as the water moccasin struck. Its scales brushed his skin but it missed. He scooped up the paddle to club it but the snake slithered over the side and into the water. He twacked the surface to scare it off, and when it didn't reappear, pulled broadside to the other boat.

The trooper had been shot in the forehead.

Fargo helped himself to the man's pack and left the man and the boat there.

For the rest of the afternoon he strained his arms and shoulders to their limit. The sun was half gone and shadows had swallowed most of the swamp when he spotted a flickering orange dot.

He pushed to reach it before nightfall. Trying to navigate the swamp in the dark would be like groping about in a room with the lights off, only deadlier.

Sunset came and went and the last faint twilight had almost faded when he came on a small island. Two boats had been dragged out of the water and tied fast. He grounded his and helped the woman and the boy out.

As campsites went, the island was ideal. It rose toward the middle to form a flat top.

A fire crackled invitingly. A coffeepot was on; the aroma made Fargo's stomach rumble.

Major Davenport and Sergeant Morgan were seated on one side. Across from them was Clementine Purdy, her head bowed, her hair disheveled.

Cleon lay near her, his head resting on a folded blanket. His left shoulder had been bandaged. He was unconscious or asleep.

The major and the sergeant and Clementine all looked as glum as could be.

Neither Fargo nor the woman and her boy made any sound. Striding into the firelight, he declared, "If I was an enemy, you'd all be dead."

Davenport and Morgan jumped up.

Clementine smiled.

"Fargo!" the major exclaimed. "Where the hell have you been? You can't imagine what we've been through."

"Let me guess," Fargo said. "Bodean and Judson tried to sneak off and strand you but one of your men caught them. They killed two troopers on the island and picked off a third later when you were chasing them. And wounded Cleon at some point."

"That's pretty much it, yes," Davenport confirmed. "They know we can't make it out of the swamp without them, and twice they've lain in ambush."

"They're playing with us," Morgan said. "They even leave signs to mark the way they've gone."

Clementine rose and came around the fire and placed her hand on Fargo's shoulder. "I'm so happy you're alive."

"Makes two of us." Fargo stepped aside and crooked a finger at the Kilatku and her son. "Remember these two?"

"You brought them back?" Major Davenport said in surprise.

"I think we're married."

"What?" Clementine said.

"How's that again?" the major asked.

"I'll tell you all about it." And Fargo did, after giving food to the woman and her son and filling a tin cup with hot coffee for himself. The only part he left out was the tit-squeezing.

"It sounds like smallpox, by God," Major Davenport said. "And you say it's wiped out most of the tribe?"

"Everyone caught it except for these two," Fargo said, with a nod at his traveling companions. "The warriors I saw were all sick. I reckon they won't last long."

"Serves them right," Sergeant Morgan said. "Going around eating people."

"What was that about being married?" Clementine brought up again. "Surely you haven't—" She blushed and didn't finish.

"I want to hear about Bodean and Judson," Fargo said.

"There's not much to tell," Major Davenport replied. "Private Lyle was keeping watch, and they stabbed him and snuck toward the boats. Private Carson woke up and yelled and gave chase, and they shot him. I imagine they intended to set all the boats but one adrift but we got there in time to stop them, and they fled. We went after them. They shot Private Esterhouse about noon. Two hours ago they shot Cleon. And here we are."

"They lie in wait and ambush us, the cowards," Sergeant Morgan fumed.

"Cleon has lost a lot of blood," Clementine mentioned. "We've done what we can for him. I'm worried infection has set in."

"We'll push on to Suttree's Landing at first light," Major Davenport told her. "With our scout to guide us, we're no longer at the mercy of those swamp rats."

"It won't be me guiding you," Fargo set him straight, and nodded at the Kilatku mother. "It'll be her."

"She'll do that for us?" Davenport skeptically asked. "You trust her enough?"

"She brought me this far," Fargo said. He didn't add that by squeezing her tit, he had the impression she considered him hers.

"Those swampers will do all they can to stop us," Davenport said. "And no doubt blame our deaths on the Kilatku." He wearily rubbed his eyes. "I was a fool to trust them. Good men paid for my folly."

"Don't be so hard on yourself, sir," Morgan said. "How were any of us to know?"

Off in the swamp an alligator bellowed and was answered by another.

"I propose we turn in early," Davenport said. "We'll take turns standing guard. Who wants the first watch?"

Fargo took the last. He was bone tired and fell asleep within moments. It felt as if he hadn't rested ten minutes when a hand was on his arm, shaking him.

"Up and at 'em," Sergeant Morgan whispered. "It's been quiet." He paused. "Well, no less than usual."

Fargo heard what he meant.

On all sides rose a discordant bedlam. The gators, the frogs, the insects, the screaming panthers and squealing wild boars and more, filled the night with a hair-prickling reminder that all around them creatures were being ripped and rent and eaten.

Fargo filled his tin cup with coffee and let the fire warm him. It took half a cup before he felt halfway alert.

He got up to stretch his legs and was pacing back and forth when someone croaked his name. He went around the fire.

"You're back," Cleon said.

"How do you feel?" Fargo asked, and hunkered. "Anything I can get you?"

"I'd be awful grateful for some water."

Fargo fetched another cup and filled it from a canteen. He held it to Cleon's lips and let him sip. "Anything else?"

"They shot me," Cleon said. "My best friends put a slug in me."

"Bastards will be bastards."

"You don't understand," Cleon said. "We grew up together. When we were kids we played together, swam together. We hunted and fished together. We'd go coon huntin' at night. They were like brothers to me and they shot me." Overcome by emotion, he broke off.

"Why talk about it if it upsets you?"

"I need to get it off my chest," Cleon said. "I'm tryin' to figure out how I could have been so wrong about them."

"It happens."

"I'd have given them the shirt off my back and they know it. I reckoned they'd always do the same for me."

"Now you know."

Cleon didn't seem to hear him. "They turned on me so easy. All because I wouldn't help them get back at you by strandin' you and these others."

"They have a reckoning coming."

"I won't hurt no woman. I told them that. They said we were just leavin' her, and I said it was the same thing because none of you would make it out alive without a boat."

"What did they say to that?"

"They called me a weak sister. Accused me of sidin' with outsiders against my own kind. Said as how if I stood up for you, I deserved the same as you."

"That sounds like Bodcan talking."

"It was him but Judson agreed. They've always been two peas in a pod, them two. Me, I was just the shell. I see that now."

"Maybe you should rest," Fargo advised.

"They tricked me. After Judson had his eye put out, he told me that he'd changed his mind. That it taught him a lesson. Him and Bodean, both, gave me their word they were goin' to see it through. But it was a trick so I wouldn't keep watchin' them. I fell asleep and slept like a baby until that trooper hollered and all hell broke loose."

Cleon closed his eyes and Fargo figured he would drift off but in a few moments he opened them again.

"They'll keep at it until all of us are dead."

"I figured as much."

"They know all sorts of tricks. One is to cut a reed and wait under the water. Another is to plaster mud and stuff all over them so they look like part of the swamp. They can be devils when they want to be."

"They're not the only ones."

"I never realized how vicious they are. How could I have been so blind?"

"We all make mistakes."

"I'm so cold," Cleon said, and his teeth chattered. "I can't feel my arm."

"I'll take a look at it when the sun comes up."

Cleon closed his eyes again. His breathing became heavier.

Fargo took that as a sign he had fallen asleep and went to rise.

"Don't let them get their hands on her," Cleon said quietly.

Fargo didn't need to ask which her he meant.

"I know them. They won't kill her outright. They'll want to have their fun first. They'll do things even a whore wouldn't let them do."

"Over my dead body."

"You're a good man, Fargo," Cleon said. "You'd do to roam the swamp with."

"You couldn't get me drunk enough."

Cleon chuckled, weakly. "It's funny how life turns out, ain't it?"

Fargo didn't answer.

"Here I am, shot by two men I trusted more than anyone."

"The only one I fully trust is my horse. And you're not dead yet."

Cleon opened his eyes and locked them on Fargo's. "Promise me," he said. "Give me your word that you'll snuff their wicks."

"The only way they'll reach the settlement," Fargo said, "is if the dead can get back up and walk."

18

Fargo tried his best. He gestured. He used sign language. He drew in the dirt. He tried every way he could think of to get the Kilatku mother to understand that he wanted her to lead them out of the swamp.

At one point her eyes widened and she bobbed her head as if she savvied, but then she swept her arm and rattled on about he-knew-not-what.

Clementine was listening, and cleared her throat. "Do you know what I think? I think she's saying that she doesn't know how."

"That's preposterous," Major Davenport said. "She's lived in this swamp her whole life."

"*Deep* in," Clementine said. "Where no one ever goes. It could be her people never come out this far."

Fargo hadn't considered that but it made sense.

"We've wasted enough time trying to persuade her," Davenport said, glancing at the sky. "The sun is up and we should be on our way."

The boats were already loaded, their fire extinguished.

Fargo and the mother and son would be in one, the major and the sergeant and Clementine and Cleon in another. They were leaving the third boat behind.

Cleon was so weak they had to carry him. Fargo had examined him at daybreak and found that infection had indeed set in. It would be a wonder if he lived out the day.

Fargo volunteered to take the lead. He had a keener sense

of direction, and with the woman to help, stood a better chance of not getting lost.

As they were about to shove off, Clementine came over. "I've changed my mind. I'd rather go with you."

About to step into the other boat, Major Davenport scowled. "Nonsense, my dear. He has the squaw. Besides, we need you to look after Cleon."

"Sergeant Morgan is better at doctoring than I am," Clementine said. "And the squaw, as you call her, is so small, she can't hardly lift a paddle."

"I insist you go in ours."

"Insist all you want. I'm going with Skye."

"You'll be out in front where the danger is greatest." Davenport refused to let it drop.

"Be that as it may," Clementine said, bending to help Fargo push out his boat, "I'll be in this one."

Fargo stayed out of their argument. He agreed with Davenport that she was taking a risk but she was a grown woman and could do as she pleased, and he wouldn't mind her help paddling.

Mother and son sat in the bow, their arms around one another.

"I have a confession to make," Clementine said as they cleared the island and entered a channel. "I didn't do this just to help you."

"You want to ask the Kilatku her recipe for stuffed white man?"

"Goodness, no. I came with you because I'm sick of the major's advances."

"He's not the perfect gentleman?"

"Oh, no, in that regard he's fine. It's just that he hovers over me so, and keeps dropping hints. I've made it plain I'm not interested but he doesn't seem to know how to take no for an answer."

"Men," Fargo said.

Up ahead the snout and head of an alligator broke the surface.

"Look at the size of that thing," Clementine gasped.

Fargo stopped paddling and reached for the Henry but the gator sank from sight with barely a ripple. His skin crawled as they passed over the spot and he watched to be sure it didn't come after them or attack the other boat.

"When I get back to Washington," Clementine remarked, "I'm going to treat myself to a pair of alligator shoes. I hear they're quite popular in Florida and some other Southern states."

The rest of the morning was uneventful—for the Archaletta. Nothing tried to eat them. Nothing tried to bite them. Once some herons took noisy wing but that was all.

Fargo kept his eyes skinned for sign of Bodean and Judson. That they didn't try to pick him off didn't lull him into thinking they wouldn't. They were waiting for the right time, the right place.

"Your friend has been awful quiet," Clementine commented.

Which was an understatement; the Kilatku mother hadn't moved or spoken since they broke camp.

"Maybe it's me," Clementine said. "She doesn't like I'm in your boat."

Fargo hoped not. The last thing he needed was a jealous cannibal.

"Have you noticed how she can't take her eyes off of you?"

"You can shut up about her now," Fargo said.

"Prickly, are we? But it's obvious she's smitten."

"Women," Fargo said.

"I don't blame her," Clementine said. "It's your own fault for being so handsome."

Fargo looked at her. "Are you dropping hints like the major?"

"I certainly am not. I was merely suggesting that if you

wanted to give your little Indian woman a tumble, she wouldn't say no."

"I don't know where her mouth has been."

Clementine laughed. "I must say, being in your boat is a lot more fun than being in the major's."

"If it's fun you want," Fargo said, "go for a walk with me tonight."

"I couldn't."

"I'll find a safe spot."

"In this swamp? With the snakes and alligators and spiders and the rest?" Clementine shook her head. "I'd be too nervous."

"I know ways to relax you."

"I bet you do."

They left it at that.

When the sun was directly overhead they stopped to rest, the two boats floating side by side.

"I can't tell you how glad I'll be when we are out of this horrid place," Major Davenport commented while mopping his sweaty brow. He smiled at Clementine. "How about if you ride with us the rest of the day to brighten my mood?"

"I'm fine as I am," Clementine responded.

"As you wish," Davenport said. "But I'm surprised you don't care that Cleon is in a bad way."

"I'm doin' all right," Cleon croaked.

He was lying. His neck above the wound looked to be swollen and discolored and his face was as white as that snow Fargo had daydreamed about. His arm below the wound appeared to be swollen, too, and he was sweating a lot worse than any of them.

"Let me have a look at you," Clementine said.

Fargo and the sergeant steadied the boats as she clambered from one to the other. She placed her palm to Cleon's forehead and gasped. "Oh my God." Very carefully, she pried at the bandage, bent, and grimaced. "The infection is spreading."

"I feared as much, my dear," Major Davenport said.

"We need to stop so I can boil water and dress the wound again."

"Look around you," Davenport said. "There isn't a spot of dry land in sight."

At the moment they were amid ranks of mossy cypress. Except for the trees, there was water everywhere.

"Then the first dry land we come to, we must stop," Clementine insisted. "Otherwise, this poor man might not make it to the settlement."

Sergeant Morgan said to Fargo, "We have another problem. I think we're being followed."

"Nonsense," Major Davenport said. "You've been saying that all morning and I haven't seen or heard a thing."

"It's a feeling I have," Morgan said to Fargo. "I can't shake it."

Fargo appreciated the warning. He wasn't as ready to dismiss it as the major. Morgan had been in the army for more than a decade; he wasn't prone to nervous fits.

"Could Bodean and Judson have slipped in behind us somehow?" Clementine asked.

"Anything is possible, ma'am," Sergeant Morgan said.

"Come now," Major Davenport said. "Don't worry her needlessly. They'll stay in front of us and ambush us when we least expect."

"That's worrisome enough," Clementine said.

Fargo offered water from the canteen to the mother and the boy. They each took a single sip. He also gave them a piece of his jerky that they ravenously ate.

"We should get under way," Davenport declared. "The more miles we cover, the sooner we're out of this mess."

Clementine frowned and looked at Fargo as if to say she was sorry about the next words that came out of her mouth. "I better stay with Cleon. But that means Skye has to handle his boat by himself."

Davenport could barely contain his delight. "It can't be helped, my dear."

"I'll help you paddle, major, if you'll let Sergeant Morgan go with Skye," Clementine said.

Davenport didn't hesitate. "You heard the lady's suggestion, Sergeant."

Morgan switched boats. If he resented being a pawn in the major's romancing of Purdy, he didn't show it.

The cypress went on for miles.

Fargo didn't recollect passing through so many on their way in. They were heading in the right direction, though, and that was what counted.

Out of the blue Sergeant Morgan said, "For what it's worth, I don't like how the major treats you."

"He's in love," Fargo said.

"He thinks his rank impresses her. He told me as much."

"He has to impress her with something," Fargo quipped. "A pecker the size of a pencil won't do it."

Morgan chuckled. "Ever notice how the self-important ones always puff themselves up?"

"That, and they love mirrors."

Grinning and nodding, Morgan said, "I've seen a side to him I never suspected. He's not the man I thought he was."

"This hellhole wears on all of us."

Morgan glanced across. "We both know he's in over his head. He was assigned to escort Miss Purdy not because he was the best officer for the job. He has friends in Washington, and he saw this as a way to boost his career."

Fargo thought of Clementine's remarks about her own career, and said nothing. He scanned the cypress ahead for openings wide enough for their boats and caught a bright flash high in a tree. "Look out!" he cried.

The next moment a rifle boomed.

19

Sergeant Morgan was flung back as if by an invisible hand.

In a twinkling Fargo had the Henry to his shoulder. He centered on a silhouette, thumbed back the hammer, and fired.

A sharp cry pierced the swamp. The silhouette separated from the bole and fell, but only a short way. Clutching a limb, it swung around to the far side of the trunk.

Fargo jacked the lever to feed another cartridge into the chamber. He waited, hoping for another shot, but the bushwhacker didn't reappear.

The woman and the boy had flung themselves to the bottom of the boat, the mother with her body over her son, shielding him.

As for Morgan, he half hung over the side, his face twisted in pain, a stain spreading on his shirt.

Quickly, Fargo pulled him in and steered the boat behind a tree wide enough to offer some protection. Setting down the Henry, he said, "Let me have a look."

Morgan's big hand was over the wound. Grunting, he moved it. "Damn me, anyhow. I should have spotted him."

The other boat thumped against theirs.

"How bad is he?" Major Davenport asked.

"Don't know yet," Fargo said. "Watch the trees." He helped Morgan slide out of the blood-soaked sleeve. The slug had penetrated below Morgan's collar bone and left an exit hole the size of a walnut. But there was good news, too. "The bone's not broken and you're not bleeding much."

"We need to dress it," Clementine said, "or it will get infected, like Cleon's."

"There has to be dry land somewhere," Major Davenport said.

They hurried on, never knowing when another shot might shatter the stillness.

For a while Morgan helped paddle one-handed but his strength gave out.

Then their luck seemed to change. A low hummock, sparse of rank growth, marked the end of the trees. Fargo brought his boat in and hopped out. He gave Morgan a hand, and pulled the boat high enough that it wouldn't drift.

Clementine bandaged the sergeant and cleaned and redressed Cleon's wound.

While she was occupied, Major Davenport crooked a finger at Fargo and walked to the end of the hummock, out of earshot.

"I want your honest assessment."

"We're in deep shit," Fargo said.

"I concur. It will slow us down even more with the sergeant wounded. So I've been thinking."

"I'm listening."

"What if you and I and Miss Purdy were to go on ahead? Without the extra weight we can make good time. When we reach the settlement we'll send help back for Sergeant Morgan and the swamper."

Fargo stared.

"What?" Davenport said. "We'll leave food and water for Morgan and Cleon and the Kilatkus."

"You'd really do that?" Fargo said, making no attempt to hide his contempt.

"I have to think of the greater good, of what's best for everyone," Davenport said. "They'll only slow us down."

"We're not leaving anyone behind."

"Perhaps I should have made myself clear," Davenport said. "I wasn't asking your opinion. I'm in command and you'll do as I say, and I say that the three of us are taking one of the boats and going for help, and that's that."

"No," Fargo said, "we're not."

"Excuse me?"

"When we go, they go with us."

"You overstep yourself. You don't have the authority to countermand my orders."

Fargo patted the Henry. "Sure I do."

Davenport turned the color of a beet. "Have a care. I can see to it that the army never hires your services again. Or better yet, I can have you thrown in a stockade."

"You'll be in there with me once General Powell hears what you've done."

Davenport considered that and adopted a friendlier tone. "Why be at loggerheads? If you're that worried about them, you can stay and Miss Purdy and I will go on alone."

Behind Davenport the water rippled.

Fargo said nothing.

"Cat got your tongue?" the major said.

A pair of eyes and a snout broke the surface. Then the ridges that ran down the reptile's broad back.

"Fine," Davenport said curtly. "Be childish. Miss Purdy and I are going on and there's not a thing you can do about it."

The alligator glided in closer, not making a sound.

"Say something, damn you."

Fargo debated, and slowly pointed. "Behind you," he said.

"Eh?"

Major Davenport started to turn just as the gator hurtled out of the water. Davenport bleated, his cry punctuated by the snap and crunch of the gator's jaws on his leg. He screamed as he was slammed onto his back and dug in his elbows to keep from being pulled into the water.

Fargo put a slug between the brute's eyes. Once, twice, a third shot, and the gator went into a roll there on dry ground.

Davenport shrieked, rolling with it.

Darting in, Fargo jammed the Henry against the gator's head and fired one more time.

The alligator opened its jaws, took a few steps into the water, and collapsed.

Davenport was out cold. His left leg was badly mangled and bleeding profusely.

Hooking his hands under the major's arms, Fargo hauled him toward the others.

Morgan, despite his wound, came to help. So did Clementine. The three of them staunched the blood with wads cut from a blanket and Clementine cleaned the wound and bandaged it.

By then the sun was high in the afternoon sky.

Fargo decided to stay there for the night. Neither the major nor Cleon were in any shape to be moved. Morgan could get around, but slowly. He wouldn't desert them, as Davenport had been so willing to do.

Since the hummock was bare of trees, Fargo stepped into a boat to go for firewood. The woman and her boy climbed in with him.

Except for the insects, the swamp was unnaturally quiet. Fargo suspected that Bodean and Judson were nearby, waiting their chance.

A dead cypress leaning low to the water was a godsend. He piled enough broken branches that it would last them the night.

As they were heading back, the woman squatted next to him, took his hand off the paddle, and placed it on her breast.

"Is that all you think about?" Fargo said. He wished he knew why she kept doing it.

The woman smiled and wriggled her hips.

Hoping he didn't hurt her feelings, Fargo removed his hand. "If it wasn't for those damn teeth . . ."

She sat back and held her son and stared accusingly at him until they reached the hummock.

Major Davenport had revived and Clementine had propped him on a pack. "I hate this swamp more than I've ever hated anything."

At last, something they agreed on, Fargo reflected.

"You were lucky not to lose your leg."

"I might as well have," Davenport said bitterly. "I can't walk. I'm of no use."

"You can paddle."

"True. Which is why I want to carry through on my original idea."

"You and her, alone?"

"Damn it, man. It's the best chance we have. We can be at Suttree's Landing by this time tomorrow."

"If you don't get lost."

"We won't if you come with us."

"How many times do I have to say no?" It took all of Fargo's self-control not to hit him. "We all go or we all stay, and you don't have a say."

"Impudent bastard," Davenport muttered. "Do you know what I think?" He struggled onto his elbows. "I think you knew that alligator was behind me. I think you didn't say anything until it was too late. I think I might be crippled the rest of my life because of you. What do you say to that?"

"I think you should learn when to keep your mouth shut."

"I was wrong," Davenport said. "There *is* something I hate more than the swamp."

"Go to hell."

Fargo got a fire going. He placed coffee on and tried to sit back and relax but it was impossible.

Cleon was asleep and mumbling in the delirium of fever. Major Davenport soon drifted under, as well. Sergeant Morgan tossed and turned.

"It's ironic, isn't it?" Clementine said, sitting across from him. "We came all this way for nothing. Disease solved the government's problem for them. Now they can finish their survey undisturbed."

"Good for them."

"Please be nice. I can't take you being surly on top of everything else."

Fargo got up and walked the perimeter of their sanctuary. He was uneasy. The sun would set soon and he didn't relish another night in that hell. He counted on their fire to keep the wild creatures at bay but it would also tell Bodean and Judson where they were.

"Was it something I said?" Clementine asked, falling into step.

"I'm restless," Fargo confessed.

"Aren't we all? I can't stand still for more than five minutes."

Only halfheartedly, Fargo joked, "I know a cure for that."

"Do you, indeed?"

"Wait until everyone falls asleep and I'll show you," Fargo said.

To his delight, Clementine coyly smiled and whispered, "I've been thinking, and I might just take you up on that." She winked, brushed her arm against his and walked back to the fire, her hips swaying more than he had ever seen them sway.

Fargo stared at the red sun and then out over the watery deathlands and finally at the lovely vision grinning invitingly over her shoulder at him.

"Son of a bitch."

20

The best-laid plans of mice and plainsmen, Fargo told himself.

It was pushing midnight. Sergeant Morgan had never gone to sleep and Major Davenport had woke up and was propped on a pack.

Cleon was still out and his forehead was a hot coal to the touch.

The Kilatku woman and her son had been asleep for about an hour.

As for Clementine Purdy, she was losing her effort to stay awake, and kept nodding off. When her chin sank to her chest for about the tenth time, she snapped her head up, yawned, and said regretfully, "I suppose I better turn in. I can't keep my eyes open."

"I can't sleep at all," Davenport said. "The pain is keeping me awake."

"I'll sit up with you, sir," Sergeant Morgan offered. "Fargo, you might as well catch some shut-eye. I'll wake you about three."

Fargo looked at Clementine. "Two would be better." If the rest were asleep, he still might have a chance.

"It's a quiet night for once," she said as she prepared her blankets. "For the swamp, anyhow."

That it was. Few gators bellowed. Few frogs croaked. The insects, too, were strangely absent.

The sky was clear, and a crescent moon added its light to the myriad of stars.

Fargo lay and admired them until sleep claimed him. He didn't dream, or if he did, he didn't remember it when he was awakened.

"It's two, according to the major's watch," Morgan informed him.

Davenport was still up.

Fargo hid his disappointment and filled his tin cup with much needed coffee. He sat cross-legged and was taking a sip when he realized that the swamp was completely still. Not a single sound emanated from the wellspring of terror.

"Peculiar, isn't it?" Davenport said when Fargo raised his head and cocked it to one side. "Everything fell silent about half an hour ago."

"I sure can't explain it, sir," Morgan said as he pulled a blanket to his chest. He yawned and closed his eyes. "I'm bushed."

Good, Fargo thought. That left the major, who was doing his share of yawning, too.

"I wish I hadn't agreed to this mission," Davenport said. "It hasn't turned out anything like I hoped it would."

Fargo didn't respond. He figured if he stayed quiet, the sooner the major would drift off.

"If my leg doesn't heal, I imagine I'll be assigned to a desk job. That would drive me crazy. I'm a man of action."

Fargo bit off a laugh.

"Yes, sir," Davenport said. "Our lives never proceed as smoothly as we'd like. How about you? Have any of your dreams ever been shattered?"

Fargo would be damned if he'd answer.

"Don't care to talk about it? I can't say I blame you." Davenport closed his eyes and pulled his hat over them. "Wake me at first light, if you would be so kind."

"First light," Fargo said.

Soon Morgan was snoring, and by the rise and fall of the major's chest, he'd fallen asleep, too.

Fargo would give them a while before he woke Clementine. He refilled his cup and settled back. The quiet was nice. For a brief span the swamp was at peace.

He'd never have thought it possible.

The fire dwindled until only a few flames licked the air. He didn't add more fuel.

Starlight and moonlight combined to cast the swamp in eerie relief. The water had a preternatural sheen.

When Fargo heard a faint splash, he assumed it was an alligator. He went on savoring the peaceful atmosphere until something moved at the limit of his vision, something low to the water. Another gator, he reckoned. From now on they were high on his list of critters he could do without, like rattlesnakes and scorpions.

Fargo turned his head and saw a second something moving toward their patch of dry ground. He looked the opposite way and there was a third.

Alarmed, Fargo set down his cup and placed his hand on his Colt. Whatever the things were, they had two to three humps. They were like no animal he'd ever seen.

He was about to rise and move to the water's edge when one of the humps unfurled.

With awful clarity, Fargo perceived the truth. The long, low things weren't animals; they were logs. The humps were men.

Even as it dawned, all the humps sat up. Their pale, splotched skin, their small size, the knives and clubs in their hands—Fargo's blood became ice and for a moment he was too stunned to shout.

Then the first log bumped dry ground, and Fargo shattered his paralysis to holler, "The Kilatku! The Kilatku are attacking!"

That was all he could get out before three of the diseased people-eaters rushed him. In the pale light they seemed more like apparitions born of demented nightmare than flesh and blood, but there was nothing fantastical about their flint knives and their clubs or their pointed teeth.

Fargo leaped to his feet. He drew and fanned a shot at a charging pale troll and the slug smashed the cannibal to the earth. Another slashed with a blade and he sidestepped, only to narrowly avoid having his ribs staved in by the club of a third.

Another log landed, and then one more. The Kilatku rushed the camp.

Yells and a scream pierced the air. The others were awake, and fighting. A gun cracked. A club thudded and someone shrieked.

Fargo shot a blotched face. He spun and shot another. Arms wrapped around his lower legs and he tried to wrest free but his own movement caused him to stumble and trip and the next second he was on the ground with not one but two Kilatku on top of him. He gripped a wrist to keep a knife from biting deep, slammed the Colt against the second cannibal.

Hissing, the Kilatku with the knife sought to stab him.

Fargo jammed the Colt against the man's chest, and fired. It folded his attacker in half and he kneed him in the head and sent him sprawling. As he rose, his hip was struck a jarring blow that nearly drove him to his knees. Twisting, he shot a warrior with a club.

For an instant he was free of attackers. Glancing about him, he beheld the grim tableau in all its grisly horror.

A bone-handled knife jutted from Cleon's chest. The Kilatku woman wouldn't be putting his hand on her tit ever again; her skull had been crushed. Sergeant Morgan was grappling with a pair of diminutive warriors who fought as fiercely as men three times their size. Major Davenport struggled with another.

Fargo didn't see the Kilatku boy—or Clementine Purdy.

Then she screamed.

A warrior was trying to pull her toward a log and she was resisting mightily. But small as he was, the man proved stronger, and in another few steps he would have her there.

Fargo aimed and blew out the warrior's brains.

A death rattle caused him to whirl.

Major Davenport had been stabbed in the throat. His hands over the wound, he tried to speak as a dark fountain gushed from his mouth and his neck. His eyes found Fargo's just as life faded.

Fargo heard a grunt and a blow.

The warrior who stabbed the major had joined the pair attacking Morgan. Morgan's left arm was next to useless, and between the three of them, the warriors were forcing him down.

The Colt was empty. In a bound Fargo reached the Henry. He shoved the Colt into his holster, scooped up the rifle, and shot the Kilatku who had stabbed Davenport. The other two were so intent on killing Morgan that they were ducks in a barrel; he put a slug into the head of one and then the other.

A splash drew his gaze to the water. A log was moving away. On it were the last warrior and the boy.

Fargo jerked the Henry to his shoulder. The warrior looked back and he aimed at the man's face. At the same moment, the boy hugged the warrior.

Fargo didn't shoot. He slowly lowered the Henry as the log faded into the swamp.

Bodies covered the ground.

Clementine was on her knees, crying.

Morgan lay on his back, a hand to his side, groaning.

Fargo went to Clementine first and hauled her to her feet. "You need to get hold of yourself."

"But—" she said, and sniffled. "That one almost—" She stopped.

"You're safe," Fargo said, and steered her toward Morgan. "Take deep breaths until you calm down."

Clementine nodded and did but she couldn't stop weeping.

"The major?" Morgan asked them, turning his head.

Fargo shook his own.

"I should have protected him." Morgan coughed and crimson speckles came out his nose.

"How bad?" Fargo asked, squatting.

"A knife in the ribs," Morgan said. "I think it punctured a lung."

"Damn," Fargo said.

"I know." Morgan coughed some more, and tried to sit up. "Help me," he requested.

Fargo got a pack and slid it behind him and helped prop him. "Anything else I can do?"

"Just stay with me until it's over."

"Until what's over?" Clementine asked. She was dabbing her eyes and nose and sniffling.

"Me," Sergeant Morgan said.

"Oh, God. Not you, too?" Clementine burst into fresh tears.

Morgan looked down at the blood seeping between his splayed fingers. "Never thought I'd die in a swamp."

"I'll bury you," Fargo said.

"With what? Your bare hands?" Morgan pressed his forearm to his mouth and coughed into his sleeve. "It would take half the day. It's best you push on." He nodded at Clementine. "You have Miss Purdy to think of."

"I'll get her out or die trying."

Morgan nodded and smiled an odd little smile. "I'm weak as a kitten. It won't be long." He held up his other hand and Fargo gripped it.

"Thanks," Morgan said, and died.

21

In the Rockies, sunrise was spectacular. Brilliant hues of pink, orange and yellow nearly always heralded the new day.

Not the swamp. The sky was a soup of clouds. A shadowy pall hung over the tangles of vegetation and the tainted water.

Fargo sat and watched a heron snatch a fish. When the great bird flapped its wings and flew aloft, he envied it its ability to fly unhindered and not have to slog through the morass of muck and reptilian monsters.

The cheek that had rested on his leg for hours now moved and Clementine Purdy stirred and opened her eyes. Sitting bolt upright, she glanced fearfully about at the bodies.

"You're safe," Fargo assured her. "You have nothing to worry about." Which was a bald-faced lie but he didn't want her to burst into tears again.

"Goodness," Clementine said. "I shouldn't have dozed off on you."

"It was the middle of the night," Fargo said. "You were tired."

Clementine stared aghast at Sergeant Morgan and at Cleon. "It's all coming back to me. Those poor men. They even killed that poor little woman who was so fond of you. And she was one of their own."

"We'll fix breakfast and head out." Fargo had no desire to linger longer than was necessary. Flies would soon swarm. Buzzards would circle and give their position away.

"I'm not really hungry," Clementine said. "Coffee will do."

Fargo was happy to oblige. He rarely started a day without a cup or three. As he went about making it, she fussed with her hair and her dress.

"Do you think we've seen the last of them?"

"The Kilatku?"

"Who else?"

"Yes." Fargo thought of the two swamp rats who wanted him dead. "But we're not out of danger yet." Far from it.

"If we can only make it to the settlement. The first thing I'll do is fill a tub with hot water and take a long bath."

"I'd like to see that."

"Me taking a bath?"

"You naked."

"I will say one thing for you. When you get an idea into your head, it stays there."

While the coffee brewed, Fargo placed all their packs in the boat he'd been using. The same with the food, canteens, everything. He also stripped the dead of their weapons.

"It's a shame we can't take the body of a Kilatku back," Clementine remarked.

"What the hell for?"

"No one has ever seen one. It would be quite a sensation."

"Aren't you forgetting something?" Fargo said, and motioned at a nearby warrior covered with loathsome blotches.

"Oh," Clementine said.

Fargo was glad to put the site of the near-massacre behind them. For a while they glided along a tranquil channel. Then it was imminent death as usual, with a network of bogs and quicksand and dark pools.

Clementine stayed quiet, much to his relief. Few things annoyed him more than having his ear bent with senseless prattle. But he should have known it wouldn't last.

"So tell me, what's the first thing you'll do when we get back?"

"Get drunk."

"Perhaps I'll join you after I take my bath."

"Or you can stay in your room with your clothes off and I'll join you."

"You never give up, do you?" Clementine asked with a grin.

"Live longer that way."

"Which reminds me," Clementine said, anxiously peering about. "Do you think we've seen the last of Bodean and Judson?"

Fargo was honest with her. "No."

"What do they hope to gain? We don't have enough money to make robbing us worthwhile."

"They're out for blood and only blood."

"All because you stood up to them and did what was right." Clementine shook her pretty head. "That's not fair."

Fair, Fargo had found, was one thing life wasn't.

She lapsed into silence and for the better part of an hour they toiled at navigating the treacherous maze. He would have gone on a while longer but she raised her paddle out of the water and set it beside her, saying, "I'm sorry. I'm not used to this. My shoulders are killing me. Can wc rest a bit?"

Fargo's answer was to place his own paddle down.

"Thank you." Grimacing, Clementine rubbed her right shoulder and then her left. "I can't wait to reach Suttree's Landing."

Fargo listened with half an ear. He was probing the swamp ahead for sign of Bodean and Judson.

Clementine did more fussing with her dress, which was matted and rumpled and bore streaks of dirt. "I must look a sight."

"We're in a swamp."

"That's no excuse. I'll look a lot more attractive with clean clothes."

"Even more with no clothes."

"Like a dog worrying a bone," Clementine said, and grinned.

Fargo stared at her bosom. "Bone, hell. I'd rather worry your tits."

"Let's not be crude. I don't know if I like being treated like a trollop."

"Ladies like to do it as much as tarts."

"Oh, do they, indeed?" Clementine said. "You must think you're an expert on the female gender."

"I've poked a few."

"Please," Clementine said, coloring. "No more of this frank talk. I don't know as I can take it."

"You're too damn timid."

"About *that* I am. I was taught it's something a lady never, ever talks about. Not even in the privacy of her bedroom."

"People," Fargo said, "do the stupidest things." Or didn't do them, as the case may be.

"It's easy for you to judge. But who's to say your scruples are better than anyone else's?"

"Never claimed they were."

Clementine bowed her head and sighed. "Sorry. I'm irritable. It's this muggy swamp and all the damn bugs."

"Did you just swear?"

She laughed, and Fargo was about to lean across and kiss her on the lips when there was a thunk on the side of the boat.

A middling-sized gator had risen from the depths. It stared at them, flicked its tail, and swam away.

"I thought it was going to attack us," Clementine said breathlessly.

So had Fargo, for an instant there.

"It never ends," Clementine said. "I'm experiencing a nightmare but I'm wide awake."

"How about we push on?" Fargo suggested. "Are your shoulders up to it?"

"Let's find out."

With every mile, the likelihood of an ambush rose. Bodean and Judson couldn't let them reach the settlement, not when Bodean and Judson's necks were as good as in a noose if that happened. He figured they would play it safe and use their rifles from a distance.

It wasn't long after they resumed paddling that Fargo spied smoke. Not a lot. Enough to suggest a small campfire.

"Look there," he said, and pointed.

"Is it them, you think?"

"Let's find out." Fargo would love to turn the tables and ambush *them*. He reckoned they had stopped to eat.

A cross-channel appeared, leading toward the smoke.

Soon they came in sight of a large island.

Fargo saw he was mistaken. The smoke wasn't rising from a campfire. It was coming out of a stone chimney.

"Why, it's a cabin!" Clementine exclaimed.

It stood well back from the water. Whoever built it had done a piss-poor job. The logs hadn't been trimmed and were fitted unevenly. A plank door hung at an angle. The window had no glass.

A canoe had been left broadside on dry land so it couldn't drift off.

"People, by God!" Clementine said happily. "I didn't know anyone lived out this far."

Fargo recollected being told that a few hardy souls lived off in the swamp rather than close to the Landing. Trappers, mostly. And sure enough, pelts hung on pegs on the cabin wall.

"Maybe they'll help us reach the settlement," Clementine said. "We're as good as saved."

"Don't get your hopes up."

The moment their bow touched, Fargo was out and pulling. Clementine joined him and helped. Their shoulders and hips brushed. He thought about how he would like her to shed that dress, and he was picturing her bare-assed when he turned and saw a man had stepped from the cabin and was staring at them.

"How do you do?" Clementine called out, and gave a cheery wave.

The man didn't return it. He was tall and lean, more bone than flesh, with a skeletal face. He wore a shirt and pants cobbled from a dozen hides: raccoon, possum, fox, bobcat and others. His footwear was stitched from rabbit fur. He was cradling an old long rifle and he had a knife on his hip.

"How do you do?" Clementine hollered again.

The trapper sauntered toward them. His left cheek bulged, and midway he spat a gob of brown juice. Near-black, beady eyes appraised them as if they were animals he was thinking of skinning.

Fargo had the Henry in his left hand. He placed his right on his Colt.

The man stopped and his thin lips twitched in what might be a smile. "Who might you folks be?"

Clementine introduced herself and Fargo, and didn't stop there. "We're part of a party the government sent in, and we're the only ones left. We can dearly use your help."

"Government?" the trapper said.

"Federal," Clementine informed him. "Out of Washington, D.C."

"I don't much like the government," the trapper said. "I don't much like those as work for it, either." And with that, he started to swing the muzzle of his rifle in their direction.

22

Fargo flashed his Colt out and up. At the click of the hammer the trapper imitated a cypress.

The trapper's throat bobbed. "Hold on there, mister. There's no call to be pullin' your hardware."

"Set the rifle down," Fargo commanded.

The man glanced at it as if he were unaware he was holding it. "I plumb forgot myself. I wasn't about to shoot you."

"I hope not," Clementine said.

With exaggerated care, the trapper placed his rifle on the ground. As he straightened he showed yellow teeth in a smile. "My name is Beauregard. Everybody calls me Beau."

"We're pleased to meet you, Beau," Clementine said cheerfully.

Fargo held his Colt steady.

"I must look a sight," Clementine said, and brushed at a bang. "We've had the most horrible time. Cannibals, alligators, killers, you name it."

"Cannibals?" Beau said.

"How far to Suttree's Landing?" Fargo asked.

Beau peered past him at their boat. "I reckon you can be there by tomorrow night if you push real hard."

Clementine beamed. "I can't wait."

"But you don't need to head right out," Beau said. "How about I fetch you somethin' to eat and drink."

Fargo was about to say they didn't want anything but Clementine had other ideas.

"I'd dearly love some tea. I don't suppose you have any?"

"Matter of fact, I do, ma'am," Beau said. "Chicory tea. There's some as don't like the taste 'cause they say it's too bitter. They don't know how to make it right, is all." He paused. "I happen to have some on the stove, if you're of a mind."

Clementine turned to Fargo. "Can we? Please? The rest would do my shoulders good."

Reluctantly, Fargo said, "One cup, and we're on our way."

Beau pointed at his rifle. "You're not fixin' to leave that there, are you? Bess has been in my family since my grandpa bought her."

"I'll bring it," Fargo said. He holstered the Colt.

Apparently the trapper did most of his skinning and curing at the side of the cabin. The ground was stained dark by the blood, and bits and pieces of animals lay rotting and stinking to high heaven.

"Pardon the smell," Beau said when Clementine crinkled her nose and coughed. "I don't give it no mind since I'm used to it."

"You trap for a living?" Clementine said.

"That I do, ma'am. Me and my pappy before me and his pap before him."

The inside of the cabin reeked of sweat and other odors. Pelts hung on every wall and dangled from hooks on the rafters.

"My word," Clementine said.

Fargo leaned the man's rifle near the door and stood where he could see out.

Beauregard fondled a coon hide. "Ain't she pretty? My hides are always prime. Anythin' worth doin', a man should take pride in."

"Why, I do believe you're a philosopher," Clementine complimented him.

"I don't rightly know what that is, ma'am," Beau said. "But if they skin and cure, that's me."

A small stove squatted in a corner. A kettle was on, and

Beau shuffled about looking in cabinets and drawers until he found three cups and set them on a table.

"I don't want any," Fargo told him.

"It's damn fine tea," Beau boasted. He touched the kettle. "Still warm. I had some this mornin'. Have some most every mornin'."

"You live here by yourself?" Clementine said. "No wife? No family?"

"I had me a woman once," Beau said. "A squaw gal. Her man drowned in the bottle, and he sold her to me to buy booze. Got her for fifty cents, if you can believe it."

"That's terrible."

"No, ma'am. She was a bargain. The quietest little thing you ever did see. Good cook, too. And she never put up a fuss when I poked her." Beau laughed. "She was strange, though. She'd just lie there. No matter how hard or how long I was at it, she never moved a muscle or let out a peep."

"That's enough," Fargo warned.

"I was only sayin'," Beau said. "Goes to show that you can't ever tell how a female will take to a poke."

"Pour the damn tea."

Beau frowned, and did. "Sorry I ain't got no sugar, ma'am. Don't care for sweets, myself."

"That's quite all right." Clementine sat and raised her cup and stopped with it halfway to her mouth. "When was the last time you washed these?"

"Ma'am?" Beau said, bending down. "Oh. That stain? That's nothin' but possum blood. I was carvin' one up and it spattered and I forgot to wash the cup off. It won't harm you none."

Under different circumstances Fargo might have laughed at the expression on Clementine's face as she took her first sip.

"It's actually quite good."

"Told you," Beau said. He opened another cabinet and brought over a burlap sack. "There's biscuits in here if you're hungry. Made them my own self about two months ago."

Clementine opened the sack and brought out a lump of dough speckled with mold. "You eat these?"

"Use 'em as bait, too," Beau said. "There's nothin' a coon likes better than a tasty biscuit."

Clementine nibbled, and grimaced. "I don't believe I'm all that hungry."

Fargo was keeping an eye on their boat and the swamp. So far the only sign of life had been a woodpecker.

Clementine swallowed more tea. "I can't thank you enough for your gracious hospitality."

"My what?" Beauregard said.

"For being so kind."

"Oh. Well, it ain't every day a fine lady like you stops by. You and this scout are the only visitors I've had in a month of Sundays."

"How do you know I'm a scout?" Fargo said.

"I was guessin'. Who else wears buckskins like yours?" Beau responded.

Fargo could think of a lot of people. "Someone else didn't happen to stop here before us, did they?"

"You just heard me say you two are the first in a long while."

Clementine said, "I don't see how you do it. I couldn't stand to live alone way out here."

"The swamp ain't that bad once you know its secrets," Beau said.

"What kind of secrets?"

"The habits of the critters, what they eat and where they hole up. Where to find good water. How to keep from bein' snake-bit and how to tell when a gator is about to show itself."

"You're forgetting the quicksand and the bugs and the snakes." Clementine shuddered.

"None of that ever bothered me much. I'm past sixty and I've lived here a good thirty years."

"You must have been one of the first."

"I was," Beauregard declared. "Before the Landin' was built, I was here trappin' for a livin'."

"We have a lot of swamp to cover yet," Fargo impatiently reminded Clementine.

"I know, I know," she said. "Another minute and I'll be done."

"You're welcome to rest here a spell," Beauregard said. "Might even be best for you to stay the night and get an early start." He quickly added, "It wouldn't bother me none, you sleepin' over."

"How nice of you," Clementine said.

"We're not staying," Fargo said gruffly.

Beau's features clouded. "I'm not too sure I like you, mister."

"Do I look like I give a damn?"

"You take a man's gun. You come in his house and insult him. You put on airs."

"You forgot one," Fargo said.

"Eh?"

"I hit you in the mouth if you don't shut up."

Clementine set down her cup so abruptly, tea spilled. "That will be quite enough. Beau is right. Your manners are atrocious."

"Finish your tea," Fargo said.

Clementine slowly raised the cup and slowly took a sip and slowly set it back down again, and smirked.

Beauregard chuckled.

"I apologize for how Mr. Fargo is treating you," Clementine said. "He's been under a terrible strain. All the people we were with are dead. We barely made it back ourselves."

"You don't say," Beau said.

Fargo thought he heard a sound outside. Sidling to the doorway, he poked his head out. All he saw were sparrows frolicking in a bush.

"I'm frazzled," Clementine prattled on. "I doubt I'll sleep well for months."

"You poor gal."

Clementine drained the stained cup, and sighed with contentment. "That was nice. I thank you again." She stood and came around the table. "I'm just about ready to depart if you are."

"Just about?" Fargo had half a mind to throw her over his shoulder and carry her.

Ignoring him, Clementine said to the trapper, "I don't suppose you have an outhouse?"

"No, ma'am," Beau said. "But the woods out back are right handy."

"Thank you."

They went out and Clementine went to the corner of the cabin.

"I won't be long."

"She's polite, that one," Beau remarked.

"I'm not," Fargo said. He debated going to the corner to watch Clementine but she'd only squawk about needing her privacy.

"I don't know what I did to rile you," Beau said.

"There's something about this place," Fargo said. He couldn't be more specific.

"You have good instincts, mister," Beauregard said. "Most folks have blinders on. Take your friend, for instance. She'd never in a million years guess that Bodean and Judson might be friends of mine and that I'd be glad to help them turn you into gator bait."

Fargo realized his back was to the other corner. He started to turn just as a gun barrel was jammed against his spine.

"Miss me?" Bodean said.

23

Beauregard spat more brown juice, and laughed. He relieved Fargo of the Henry and his Colt and stepped back out of reach. "Surprise."

Fargo looked over his shoulder. "I had a feeling," he said.

"I've known Beau for years," Bodean said. "Jud and me have been spyin' on you and the woman. We knew you were headed this way. So we circled in front of you and I asked Beau to lend a hand. He was happy to oblige."

"For twenty dollars," Beau said. "And you better have the money. I find out you lied, there'll be hell to pay."

"It's practically every cent I have to my name but it's worth it to pay this bastard back." Bodean jabbed his rifle harder into Fargo. "I've been thinkin' on how to do you in. I don't want it quick or easy. I want you to suffer."

"I'll lend you one of my skinnin' knives," Beau offered.

"That's somethin' a redskin would do," Bodean said. "I've got me a better notion." He stepped away and glanced at the corner Clementine had gone around. "She better not take too damn long."

Fargo was tempted to make a break for it but he'd have a slug in him before he took a step.

"Yes, sir," Bodean said, his eyes lit by vicious gleams. "I can't hardly wait."

"Don't involve me in that part, no how," Beau said. "This is betwixt you and him."

"Since when did you become skittish?"

"Since I heard they're government folks. The last thing I want is more of their kind nosin' around askin' a lot of questions."

"Hell," Bodean said. "No one knows they're here but us. The government does come lookin', these two'll be nothin' but bones."

"Leave the woman out of it," Fargo said.

"Not hardly. She'll tell about Cleon and that big soldier and we'll have the law breathin' down our necks."

Beauregard stiffened. "Hold on. What was that about Cleon?"

"They shot him," Fargo said. "The wound became infected. He couldn't fight back when we were attacked by the Kilatku and they killed him."

"The hell you say."

"Cleon turned on us, Beau," Bodean said. "He sided with the soldiers. What else were we to do?"

"I liked Cleon," Beau said. "He was a good ol' boy. You shouldn't ought to have shot him."

"I've explained how it was."

"There's no excuse for shootin' one of our own." Beau shook his head. "No, sir. His folks need to be told."

"Damn it, Beau. Use your head."

"I'll take my canoe. I'll leave you out of it. I'll just say the Kilatku killed him."

"Let Jud and me do it."

"I don't want to be here when you kill these two, anyhow," Beauregard said, and turned to go inside. "I'll fetch my rifle and head right out."

Bodean shot him in the back.

At the blast, Beau was slammed against the jamb.

He clutched it and gasped, "Why, Bodean? Why?"

"I don't know as I can trust you to keep your mouth shut," Bodean said.

Beauregard collapsed. On hands and knees he went through

the doorway and groped along the inner wall. "Where's that rifle of mine?"

"No you don't." Bodean walked up to him, held the muzzle an inch from Beau's head, and sent lead crashing through his brain.

"That's two of your own," Fargo said.

"I forgot how close Cleon and him were," Bodean said. "You had to go and mention we'd killed him, didn't you?"

There was commotion at the side of the cabin and presently Clementine Purdy stumbled into view. She had a bruise on her face she hadn't had before. Glaring behind her, she snapped, "Quit shoving me."

Judson strolled out, rifle in hand, his ruined eye covered by an eye patch cut from his shirt. "Don't give me trouble, bitch. Not in the mood I'm in." He stared at the legs jutting out of the cabin. "Beau?"

"Had to," Bodean said.

"We have to hide the body. People found out it was us, we'd be lynched."

"We'll blame it on them," Bodean said, nodding at Fargo and Clementine.

"No one will ever believe I harmed anyone," Clementine said.

"You're outsiders," Bodean said. "They'll believe anything about outsiders."

Judson motioned at the swamp. "We should get to it. Someone might happen by."

"Not likely, but we will anyway." Bodean motioned at Fargo and Clementine. "Walk toward the water. Hands where I can see them."

Fargo was ready to pounce if either of them let down their guard.

"What are your intentions?" Clementine asked.

"I aim to let the swamp take care of you."

"You're unspeakably vile."

"You brought this on yourselves, lady," Judson said, and touched his crude patch. "Your friend here should have let me kill the red brat who did this."

Fargo was racking his brain. He might jump one but the other would shoot him. He needed a distraction of some kind.

"You're lookin' mighty worried," Bodean noticed, and laughed. "In a little bit you'll be worried a lot more."

"I wouldn't want to be them," Judson said.

Fargo hated being helpless. His instinct was to fight. He scanned the swamp, hoping against hope someone from the settlement might pass by or pay the trapper a visit.

"Do you admit the truth even to yourselves?" Clementine asked the pair.

"What truth, bitch?" Bodean said.

"Cleon told us how you planned to strand the whole party. Yet now you claim we're to blame for all you've done. You're despicable."

"Keep flappin' your gums," Bodean said. "Make it worse for yourself."

"You can only kill me once."

"It's *how* we kill you that counts. You'll scream your lungs out before you die, and that's no lie."

"Sure ain't," Judson said.

Fargo came to the canoe and stopped. He couldn't imagine what the pair had in mind.

"Go left into those trees yonder," Bodean commanded. "Nice and slow."

"My only regret is that I won't get to watch you hang," Clementine said. "Texas does that with their criminals, I hear."

"Only when there's proof they broke the law," Judson said.

"In your case, bitch, there won't be a lick of evidence," Bodean said, and laughed.

The woods grew to the swamp's edge. Fargo considered grabbing Clementine's hand and making a run for it through the trees but Bodean stepped in close and pressed the rifle to his spine.

"I know what you're thinkin'. It's what I'd think if'n I was in your boots."

Ten yards in they came to a half-moon inlet fringed by grass. Water lilies covered much of the surface, hiding whatever lurked beneath.

To Fargo's consternation, stakes had been pounded into the ground, and next to each was a short coil of rope.

"We got it set up earlier," Bodean said. "Beau told us this was the best spot. You'll find out why soon enough."

"Lie down between the stakes," Judson said.

"I will not," Clementine responded, and whirling, she bolted toward the trees.

Judson was on her before she took two steps. He slammed the stock of his rifle against her temple and she crumpled like a stricken doe.

There was nothing Fargo could do. Bodean would blow his spine apart if he so much as twitched.

"You better not have killed her, Jud," Bodean said.

"I was careful," Judson said. Seizing Clementine's wrist, he dragged her over.

Bodean nudged Fargo. "Lie down, damn you. Take off that hat first."

With Judson holding a rifle to his face, Fargo was forced to submit to having his wrists and ankles tied to stakes. He worried that Bodean would take off his boot and discover the Arkansas toothpick but the swamp man looped the rope around the boot and tied the rope so tight, he couldn't move.

"Now for the government gal."

Clementine groaned as she was tied.

The pair stood back and regarded their handwork with sadistic pleasure.

"We're all set," Judson said.

"It will be somethin' to see. And if it works, folks will never suspect we had a hand in it."

Bodean squatted next to Fargo. "You're probably wonderin' why we're goin' to so much bother. It'd be a sight easier to blow your brains out or slit your damn throats."

Fargo glared.

"But like I said, we want you to suffer. And I can't think of anything that would make you suffer more than bein' ate alive."

Fargo glanced at the water lilies.

"I can guess what you're thinkin'. That there's a gator in that pool. But a gator would drag you into the water and drown you and take you to its den." Bodean shook his head. "It'd be over too quick."

"And we wouldn't get to see you die," Judson said.

"Gators ain't the only things that eats folks, though," Bodean said. "There's bears. But Beau made good money off their hides and kilt every bear he came across and there ain't any hereabouts."

"He liked cats, though," Judson said.

Bodean nodded. "He liked cats so much, he couldn't bring himself to kill the painter that lives on this island. You'd call it a mountain lion, I reckon."

"And guess where that painter comes damn near every evenin' for a drink?" Judson took up the account, and nodded at the inlet.

"Cats like to play with their prey and take their time eatin' it," Bodean said.

"And we'd get to watch," Judson said.

"We need to make sure your scent doesn't scare it off, though," Bodean said. "Painters can be skittish of people."

"That's right," Jud said. "We have to lure it in with somethin' it can't resist." He drew the knife on his hip.

"Can you guess what that is?"

24

Jud grinned and wagged the blade. "Where to cut? The neck and the wrist, you'd bleed out before the painter comes."

"We wouldn't want that," Bodean said. "How about the forehead?"

Judson tapped the tip of the blade on Fargo's brow, each tap bringing a prick of pain. "Not a bad idea."

Fargo boiled with fury.

"Right along the hair there," Bodean said.

Grinning wider, Judson cut from left to right along Fargo's hairline.

The pain wasn't as bad as Fargo thought it would be. He felt a wet sensation and suddenly blood was in both eyes. He blinked to clear them but the world was a red blur.

Judson laughed. "There. That should do it. It'll dry before the painter comes but he'll still smell it."

"Cats have good noses," Bodean said.

"Now for the bitch."

Fargo struggled to stay calm. He went on blinking and tossed his head but his vision only became worse. It struck him that if the blood did dry, he wouldn't be able to see when the cougar came.

"It's done," Judson declared.

Fargo glimpsed vague movement.

"Beau told us the painter always comes along about sundown so you have a few hours yet," Bodean said. "Think of those sharp teeth and claws while you're waitin'."

Judson laughed.

"A half hour or so before the sun goes down, we're goin' to take the canoe off a ways and watch from where we can't be seen."

"We wouldn't want the cat to catch our scent," Judson said. "Might spook it."

"Any last words?" Bodean taunted.

Fargo refused to give them the satisfaction of venting his rage.

"No?" Bodean said. "Well, I have some for you. After this is all over, we're helpin' ourselves to that stallion of yours."

"Not that we have much need for a horse to ride," Judson said.

"No," Bodean said. "We get around mainly by boat and walkin'."

"Horse meat, though, sure is tasty," Judson said, and smacked his lips.

"We'll think of you as we're roastin' your animal over our fire."

"And as we're bitin' into a juicy piece," Judson threw in.

They cackled.

Fargo listened to their footsteps fade. His right eye was still covered in blood but his left had cleared a little. Turning his head, he saw Clementine with blood over her brow; only a little had gotten into her eyes.

Coiling every sinew in his body, he tested the ropes and stakes. First one limb and then the other and then all four at once, straining with all his strength. Not one stake moved. They were imbedded deep.

Fargo sank back. Think, he told himself. He had a few hours yet. It wasn't hopeless.

Clementine moaned. She was coming around. Her whole body started and her eyes snapped open and she looked around in a panic.

"You're all right," Fargo said. "They cut you but not deep."

His voice seemed to soothe her. She blinked and shuddered and swallowed.

"Where did they get to?"

Fargo told her everything.

"A cougar is coming?" Clementine said in disbelief. "They hardly ever attack people. Do you think this one will really eat us?"

"There's no predicting." Fargo would rather not be there to find out.

"They're insane, the pair of them."

"Sons of bitches, yes," Fargo said, "but as sane as you or me."

"How can you defend them? Who in their right mind stakes human beings out for animals to eat? It's torture, pure and simple."

Fargo could have told her that Apaches and other tribes tortured their enemies all the time, and they weren't insane, either.

Clementine did as he had done and pulled at each of her stakes. "It's no use."

"We can't give up." Fargo tried again. He tried until sweat poured from every pore and his arms and legs hurt like hell. Subsiding, he gathered his strength for another attempt.

"I refuse to die like this," Clementine said. "It's humiliating."

"More so than being shot?"

"Don't patronize me. Who wants it on their headstone that they were eaten by a cougar?"

"I doubt Bodean and Judson will go to that much trouble."

"My family and friends will. They won't rest until they learn the truth. They'll find my remains and take them back East and give me a proper burial."

"If you say so."

Twice more Fargo sought to move a stake, any stake. Twice more he failed. Exhausted, he lay staring at the clouds through his one eye.

"Skye?" Clementine said softly.

Fargo grunted.

"The swamp," Clementine whispered. "God in heaven, the cougar isn't the only thing that might eat us."

Fargo raised his head. At first he didn't see what she was talking about. Then a water lily moved, and he saw the tip of a snout and the eyes of an alligator. "It's a small one. It won't bother us."

"Are you sure?"

No, Fargo wasn't, but he didn't tell her that. And where there was a small one there might be a big one.

He couldn't afford to worry about gators. He had a greater worry; namely, to get free before the painter appeared.

To that end, he grit his teeth and heaved against the stakes holding his wrists. Both had been pounded in so far, the tops of the stakes were practically flush with the ground.

But this wasn't the Rockies where the ground was as hard as iron. This was swamp soil. Soft soil. Easy to dig in. Eventually, he should be able to loosen one or both.

He concentrated on that and nothing else. He surged against the ropes until his arms and shoulders couldn't take the pain anymore, and rested a bit. As soon as the pain faded, he surged again. Over and over and over, so many times over the next couple of hours, he lost count. His shoulders grew so sore, moving them was agony. His wrists became chafed and bloody. Every muscle in his arms ached. He didn't care.

For once Clementine stayed mostly quiet. She told him when the small gator submerged. She mentioned a large snake that glided past.

The sun was a golden bowl of fire on the western horizon when she said his name.

"I can see the canoe! Bodean and Judson are going out a ways, as they said they would."

Fargo was running out of time. His body was a welter of pain. Steeling himself, he tried yet again.

The right stake moved. Not a lot. A fraction, only.

Almost fiercely, he worked it back and forth. It moved only by fractions but that was the thing with a stake. Once you moved a stake a little, it became easier. This one loosened rapidly. "Are they watching us?"

"I don't think so. They're talking and drinking from a jug."

Fargo tugged at the stake. It moved a tenth of an inch. A quarter of an inch. Then he could move it half an inch. He tugged harder, tugged until he thought he'd tear his arm from its socket, until the torment was enough to make him want to cry out. The stake rose an inch. He rested for all of thirty seconds and went at it again. The stake rose another inch. Rest. Pull. Rest. Pull. The stake rose a good five inches but it wasn't enough. "How goddamn long is this thing?" he fumed, and exerted all the strength he had left in his body.

The stake popped free.

Fargo lay back and looked at it, his shoulder throbbing. The stake was over a foot long, a straight piece of tree limb that Bodean or Judson had whittled to a point. "Where are they now?"

"Making for some reeds. I think they intend to hide there to watch. Their backs are to us at the moment."

"Good." Fargo twisted and gripped the stake that held his left arm with his right hand. He pushed, then pulled, putting all his weight into it. Pushed, pulled, pushed, pulled. This time it didn't take as long. In less than a minute the stake was loose enough that when he wrenched, it slowly rose higher until, with a gasp, he pulled it all the way out.

Exhausted, he sank back. He made sure to position his arms so that it appeared they were still tied to the stakes.

"They're in the reeds," Clementine reported. "They're turning the canoe. I can see their faces."

Fargo had done all he could for the moment. Should he try to free his legs, Bodean and Judson would likely shoot him.

"What are you waiting for?" Clementine asked. "Do me."

"Glad to," Fargo said. "Once we're out of this goddamn swamp."

"What? No. I meant pull my stakes out."

"They're watching us."

"Do it quick, before they can get here."

"They have rifles," Fargo reminded her.

"Oh." Clementine frowned. "Damn. And I have to—you know—so badly."

Fargo looked at her.

"Well, I do. My bladder isn't as strong as yours. I can't drink a cup of tea and not have to go off in the bushes."

"It's called taking a piss."

"I asked you before not to be crude."

Fargo looked at the stakes that held her, and at the swamp, and the reeds twenty yards out, and was about to tell her that "crude" was the least of her problems, when Clementine glanced past him, toward the woods, and stiffened. He knew what he would see before he turned his head.

The painter had come for its evening drink. In every respect it was a copy of the cougars that prowled the Rockies except that its coat was more gray than brown and its tail was thicker and shorter.

The thing was huge. Possibly the largest mountain lion Fargo had ever seen.

The instant he looked at it, it bared its fangs and growled.

25

"Don't make a sound," Fargo said quietly, and even though she was staked to the ground, he added, "and don't move."

Its belly brushing the grass, the cougar stalked toward him.

Fargo's mouth went dry. The only defense he had were the stakes. But if he used them, Bodean and Judson would know his arms were loose.

The cougar stopped. Its tail twitched and it tilted its head and sniffed.

A chill rippled through Fargo. The cat had smelled the blood. And it was well known that cats loved to lick blood when they devoured prey.

"Skye," Clementine whispered.

"Shut the hell up."

The cougar tensed at the sound of their voices, and snarled.

Fargo had no choice but to resort to the stakes if the thing attacked. They were the only weapons he had. Then he remembered. "Do you still have that derringer?"

"I put it in my pack," Clementine whispered, "and the pack is in the boat."

"Wonderful." Fargo thought of the Arkansas toothpick, so near to his hand and yet so far.

And then the mountain lion was next to him.

Fargo scarcely breathed.

The cat breathed, though, on his face. Warm puffs tingled his cheek. The cougar bent its head and for a few heart-stopping moments he feared it was going to sink its fangs into him.

Instead, to his amazement, its tongue flicked out and it licked the dry blood.

Clementine gasped.

The cat glanced at her and went back to licking.

Fargo held his breath. The tongue rasped like sandpaper. A few more licks and the cougar accomplished what would take five minutes of hard scrubbing; it licked his face clean.

Now, Fargo thought, it would get down to eating him.

But no. The cougar straightened and looked down at him, and purred. Just like a house cat or an alley cat. He knew that mountain lions often purred when eating, or when a mother was nursing her young.

"It likes you," Clementine whispered.

No, it liked his blood, Fargo knew, and it might have a craving for more.

Then, incredibly, the big cat turned and sauntered off into the woods without a backward look.

"Sweet Jesus," Clementine breathed.

Caked in cold sweat, Fargo moistened his mouth and swallowed. For a minute there he'd forgotten about Bodean and Judson but their angry shouts reminded him he was still in the frying pan.

"What the hell?"

"Come back here, you stupid painter! You're supposed to eat them!"

The canoe nosed out of the reeds and Bodean and Judson paddled toward shore.

"They're coming," Clementine anxiously declared.

Quickly, Fargo gripped the stakes and slid the trimmed ends into the holes. He pushed each in as far as it would go and lay exactly as Bodean and Judson had left him. They were still a good ways out and didn't appear to notice.

"What do we do?" Clementine asked.

"We kill the sons of bitches."

"I can't do a thing to help. It will have to all be you."

Fargo didn't expect otherwise. "Hush now."

The water rippled and the canoe swished through the lilies. Momentum carried it onto dry land and Bodean hopped over the side and held it while Judson climbed out.

"I don't believe it," Bodean said, facing them. "I saw it with my own eyes and I goddamn don't believe it. That stupid cat."

Judson came over to Fargo. "You're the luckiest bastard who ever lived."

"I guess there's a reason painters don't attack people much," Bodean said. "I thought for sure the blood would do the trick."

"I ever see that cat again, I'll shoot it dead," Judson said. He squatted. "But there's a sayin'. If you want somethin' done right—"

"Do it your own self," Bodean finished for him.

"There are plenty of other ways to kill you," Judson said. "We can feed you to a gator in bits and pieces."

"Or drown you," Bodean said. "Or toss you into quicksand." He came closer, holding his rifle with the barrel pointed down.

"Or maybe just shoot you and bury you," Judson said. "No one will ever find your bodies anyhow."

"I like that idea," Bodean said. "I want this over with. I want to get drunk and screw a woman and sleep for a week."

"You and me, both," Judson said. He fingered the hilt of his knife. "Any last words, mister, before we do what we should have done in the first place?"

"How does it feel?" Fargo asked.

Judson paused in the act of unsheathing his blade. "How does what feel?"

"Losing an eye?"

"We're about to turn you into worm food and you want to know a thing like that?"

"I couldn't see out of one of mine for a while and it bothered the hell out of me," Fargo said, firming his grip on the stakes. "It must have been a lot worse for you when that boy stabbed you."

"You miserable bastard."

"How will you feel about losing both?"

"Both?" Judson said.

With a powerful heave, Fargo tore the two stakes free. Sweeping upward, he stabbed Judson in his good eye, driving the stake into the socket as far as it would go. Judson shrieked and threw himself back, on top of Clementine. She screamed and bucked to get him off.

Bodean was riveted in astonishment. Belatedly, he tried to bring his rifle into play.

Fargo lunged and thrust the other stake into Bodean's left thigh. The tip penetrated several inches, and scarlet spurted.

Bodean cried out and staggered. Dropping his rifle, he clutched his leg and lurched toward the canoe.

Judson was thrashing and shrieking, "I'm blind! I'm blind!"

Fargo tried to grab the rifle but it was just out of reach. He tore at the knots to the rope binding his ankle and loosened it enough to slip his hand into his boot. A few slashes of the toothpick and he was free. He scooped the rifle up and snapped it to his shoulder but the canoe was ten yards out and Bodean was lying on the bottom. All he could see was an elbow.

"Help me!" Clementine screeched. "Get him off! Get him off!"

Judson had gone limp, blood and gore oozing from his ruptured eye, the stake in his socket jutting at the sky.

"Don't just sit there!" Clementine pleaded.

Setting the rifle down, Fargo gripped Judson's ankles and slid him off her. Judson's head flopped and blood smeared her cheek and neck and her dress. She shuddered and grimaced.

"Is he dead?" she asked. "Please tell me he's dead and get him off me."

Fargo didn't have time to spare. Bodean was getting away. Quickly, he cut the ropes binding her to the stakes.

"At last," Clementine cried, and wiped at her neck with her sleeve. "I think some of his blood got into my mouth."

"Look at the bright side," Fargo said, sliding the toothpick into its sheath. "You could have cougar spit on your face."

"Is that supposed to be funny?"

Fargo didn't answer. He was running toward the cabin. Neither of the swamp men had had his Colt or the Henry. The guns could only be one place.

"Wait for me!" Clementine hollered.

Fargo ran faster. His hunch was rewarded when he burst into the cabin and saw his pistol and rifle on the table. Scooping them up, he raced out the door.

The canoe had disappeared into the reeds.

"Hold on, will you?" Clementine yelled, moving to intercept him.

Without slowing Fargo said, "I'm going after Bodean."

"I'll go with you."

"Like hell."

Fargo reached the boat, set the Henry in, and pushed.

Clementine caught up, saying, "You're not leaving me here alone and that's final."

"It's too dangerous," Fargo said.

"He dropped his rifle," Clementine said. "You should be able to capture him easy."

"Capture, hell," Fargo said. The boat slid clear of the shore and he jumped in. He grabbed a paddle, intending to push off before Clementine could clamber on, but she was too quick for him. "Get out."

"Where you go, I go."

"Damn it, woman."

"You'll have to tie me to keep me here and he'll escape." Clementine grasped his arm. "Please, Skye. I'm afraid to be by myself."

Swearing, Fargo dipped his paddle into the water. "Lend a hand, then. But you're to do as I tell you."

"When don't I?"

They flew to the reeds. Fargo entered them at about the

same spot the canoe had. The stems rustled and crackled. Bent reeds told him which direction Bodean had gone.

"I just saw a snake," Clementine whispered.

"In a swamp?" Fargo said.

"How can you joke at a time like this? For all you know he might be waiting to kill us."

"No 'might' about it."

"Then why are we going in after him?"

"We finish it here and now."

The reeds buckled with every stroke of a paddle. A frog croaked, and something big moved noisily away.

"If I never see a swamp again," Clementine said, "it'll be too soon."

More reeds parted—and there was the canoe.

Fargo brought the boat alongside it. Blood smeared the bottom.

"Where can he have got to?"

The water exploded. Gripping the side of their boat, Bodean levered himself up and over even as he lanced his knife at Fargo's throat. Jerking back, Fargo grabbed Bodean's wrist, twisted, and shoved. Bodean grabbed his other arm. The next he knew, they were over the side and hitting the reeds with a splash.

Clementine bawled his name.

Fargo lost his hold. He braced for the searing sensation of the blade but Bodean placed both hands on his head to hold him under. The bastard intended to drown him.

Groping at his boot, Fargo resorted to the toothpick.

He drove it up and in and felt it shear flesh. The pressure on his head eased and he rolled and broke the surface.

Bodean had a hand to his side. His other hand was empty. Evidently he'd dropped his knife when they fell in.

"No," he bleated. "I beg you. You wouldn't kill an unarmed man."

"Not usually," Fargo said.

Bodean exhaled in relief.

"But in your case," Fargo went on, drawing his Colt, "I'll make an exception."

"No! Don't!"

Fargo shot him in the forehead. The body smacked the water, convulsed once, and was still. "I should have skinned him alive first," he said.

"I can't believe it's over," Clementine said. "You saved my life." She reached out to help him climb in. "How can I ever repay you?"

Fargo stared at her breasts and her thighs and the junction in between. "Three guesses," he said.

LOOKING FORWARD!
**The following is the opening
section of the next novel in the exciting
Trailsman series from Signet:**

**TRAILSMAN #376
NEW MEXICO MADMAN**

*New Mexico Territory, 1860—where Fargo serves as
bodyguard for "America's Sweetheart" on a stagecoach
bound straight for hell.*

"When I was still just a tad wearing short pants, Olney, I
found a sparrow with a broken wing. I picked it up and held
it trapped in one hand. Have you ever held a small bird captive in your fist?"

While he spoke, Zack Lomax stood in the embrasure of a
bay window looking out upon Santa Fe's fashionable College
Street. When no answer was forthcoming, he spun around suddenly to stare at his subordinate.

"Well? *Have* you, man?"

Olney Lucas glanced quickly away from those intense,
burning-coal eyes. "No, boss, I never done that."

"Well, you should try it sometime because it's an immense
thrill of power. Even as a kid I felt it—like I was God in the

universe, see? I could feel its tiny heart racing like the mechanism of a fine Swiss watch. And suddenly I realized I was the master of life and death. One good squeeze and I could cancel that sparrow's existence forever. The thrill it gave me . . . later, as a man, not even the glory of the rut can match that thrill."

Lomax laced his fingers behind his back and began pacing the fancy Persian carpet in his study. He was of middle height, built solid as a meetinghouse, and well turned out in a dark wool suit with satin facings on the lapels. His hard, angular, shrewdly intelligent face featured fiercely burning eyes of limitless ambition and brooding obsession. Eyes few men could meet for more than a second or two without being unnerved and looking away.

"I'm a man now, Olney, not a lad in short pants. And the new sparrow in my hand is a vicious, supercilious bitch named Kathleen Barton. 'America's Sweetheart.' In a pig's ass! Do you have *any* idea what that self-loving, stuck-up thespian bitch cost me?"

Olney had worked for Lomax long enough to know which questions required answers. Lomax would answer this one himself, just as he had hundreds of times since that fateful day, almost one year ago, in San Francisco.

"That goddamn election was *mine*!" Lomax fumed. "Bought and paid for. I had the Barbary Coast Hounds on my payroll and half the aldermen blackmailed. Think of it, Olney—Mayor of San Francisco! California itself was the next prize, and with slavery legalized there I would have run an empire. That ball-breaking twat cost me all of it. *All* of it! Turned me into a national laughingstock afraid to show my face in public."

For Lomax, who had never brooked a slight in his life, this was no old wound, but a fresh scab being torn off every day. He felt rage and shame searing into him anew. Plenty of men had proposed marriage to beautiful women and been given the mitten. But he had made the fatally overconfident mistake of proposing to Kathleen Barton on the front page of *The Californian*—a grandiose gesture he was sure would sweep the alluring actress off her feet.

Instead, she had ruined him every way but financially. Her scathing letter of rejection—also front-page newspaper fare—had described him as "a criminal beast who deserves public flogging" and assured her adoring public she "would rather kiss a toad than let that despicable, corrupt scoundrel ever touch me."

With one devastating letter his hopes for controlling the Bear Flag Republic were reduced to mere mental vapors. And thanks to this new Associated Press for the sharing of telegraphic dispatches, his shame and ruin had become a national—eventually even international—cause célèbre. Too humiliated to even face the society he once dominated, he'd pulled his hat from the political ring to avoid a landslide defeat.

"Well, the fancy bitch had her fun," Lomax declared now, still furiously pacing. "But you know my anthem, Olney: Whoever does not submit to the rudder must submit to the rock."

"Sure, boss. But is it such a good idea to kill her on the first anniversary of her letter? I mean, Christ! It's a fingerboard pointing right at you."

"Sell your ass. All the world knows that Zack Lomax was supposedly killed in an explosion at one of his own San Francisco breweries. Here in Santa Fe I'm Cort Bergman, mining investor. No one will even make the connection. And everyone knows that beautiful, popular theater actresses are magnets for unstable admirers. Her death will never be traced to me—except that *she* will know. I'll make damn sure of that."

Shaking off his familiar, acid-bitter rage, Lomax suddenly became all business. "You've followed my instructions to the letter?"

Olney nodded. "Russ Alcott swears by all things holy

that we can trust this informer. He's high up in Overland's New Mexico Division. Kathleen Barton used a fake name and wore a veil, but she's too famous and he recognized her. She's booked passage for the El Paso to Santa Fe run day after tomorrow."

A hard-lipped smile straight as a seam divided Lomax's face. "That rings right. Her performance at El Paso's Palacio Theater has just closed, and she's opening here in town at the Bella Union in just twelve days. Have you set up the mirror-relay system?"

"All set. Just like the army uses out here. As long as the sun's shining, you and Alcott can communicate quick as a finger snap."

Lomax looked pleased. "Any new word on special security arrangements for her?"

Olney Lucas fortified himself with a deep breath. *Stand by for the blast*, he warned himself.

"Well, you were right, boss. There'll be no military escort. Overland's Division Manager, and the bitch's agent, don't want no attention drawn to the run. Soldiers usually escort bullion runs, and they don't want to lure Mexican freebooters."

He hesitated, and Lomax alerted like a hound on point. "What is it?" he demanded sharply.

"Well, the thing of it is—according to Alcott's report, this theater agent won't be travelling with her. He's hired on Skye Fargo as the shotgun rider. Actually, as Barton's bodyguard."

For a moment Lomax looked as if he'd been slugged hard but not quite dropped. He stopped pacing, and for a full thirty seconds stood as still as a pillar of salt, his face going pale as fresh linen.

"Fargo!" He spat the word out like a bad taste. "The 'savage angel' as the fawning newspaper scribblers call him. The 'man whom bees will not sting.'"

"Maybe bees *can* sting him, but it's a hard-cash fact that he's left a trail of graves all over the West. He's hell on two sticks."

Lomax seemed to gather himself, squaring his shoulders and regaining some color in his face. "No question about it, Olney, he's no man to take lightly. In fact, if we are not meticulously careful Skye Fargo is the rock we'll split on. But I planned for something like this. For *one full year* I've worked this out."

Lomax resumed pacing like a caged tiger. "Fargo is famous for his prowess as a killer, certainly. But often he wins the day by a simple strategy: always mystify, mislead, and surprise your enemies. By a happy coincidence, that's *our* strategy, too."

Olney perked up at this reminder. "By God, it is, ain't it?"

"We're attacking our opponent at his greatest strength. And don't forget, neither Fargo nor anyone else knows we have an informer inside Overland. And wouldn't you agree that Russ, Cleo and Spider are first-rate killers?"

"Just like Fargo—no men to fool with, boss. In Lincoln County they call Russ Alcott the Widow Maker. I've seen him light matches with a pistol at twenty feet. And he handpicked those two siding him."

Lomax nodded. "Fargo can't possibly know we'll have a paid killer on that coach, too, as our ace in the hole. Or even that we know exactly *which* run Kathleen will be on. If they switch runs at the last minute, we'll know that also."

"The way you say, boss. But no matter how you slice it, there's no killing the woman until we put the quietus on Fargo. And slick plan or no, when it comes to *that* job, it'd be easier to put socks on a rooster."

Again Lomax nodded. "Never underrate your enemy. The road to hell is paved with the bones of fools who made that mistake. I won't. *One year*, Olney. Night and day, planning even for something as formidable as Skye Fargo. But the suspense clock has been set ticking: exactly eleven days from now, on June 19, 1860, Kathleen Suzanne Barton will draw her ultimate breath in this world."

He crossed to a huge mahogany desk and picked up a Spanish dagger featuring a jewel-encrusted, hammered-silver hilt.

"Fargo first, of course, and I don't give a damn who kills him or how. And then, ten miles west of this City of Holy Faith . . . at a spot appropriately named Blood Mesa. First, I'll watch the terror ignite in her eyes—make that proud, haughty beauty beg and grovel, perhaps even piss herself. Next, I'll shred that breathtakingly beautiful face, and then I'll carve her goddamn stone heart out of her chest. Just the way she cut mine out back in San Francisco."

By now Lomax was breathing so hard his breath whistled faintly in his nostrils.

"Boss?" Olney said quietly.

It took Lomax a long moment to realize his lackey had spoken. "Yes?"

"Just curious. That bird you caught when you was a kid—what happened to it?"

Lomax's lips twitched. He held one open hand out, then suddenly squeezed it into a tight fist. "Master of life and death, Olney. Just like God in the universe."

Cameron Judd
Colter's Path

When Jedediah "Jedd" Colter hears of a band of travelers bound for the gold fields of California, he uses his hunting skills to convince the Sadler brothers to hire him as a guard. While the journey is difficult and its leaders incompetent, Jedd's natural skills enable him to keep the peace and save them all from disaster.

But when he's injured along the way and the Sadlers head west without him, Jedd has only one thing on his mind—making it to California on his own and getting even with those that did him wrong…

"Judd is a fine action writer."
—*Publishers Weekly*

Available wherever books are sold or at
penguin.com

Frank Leslie

DEAD MAN'S TRAIL

When Yakima Henry is attacked by desperados, a mysterious gunman sends the thieves running. But when Yakima goes to thank his savior, he's found dead—with a large poke of gold amongst his gear.

THE BELLS OF EL DIABLO

A pair of Confederate soldiers go AWOL and head for Denver, where a tale of treasure in Mexico takes them on an adventure.

THE LAST RIDE OF JED STRANGE

Colter Farrow is forced to kill a soldier in self-defense, sending him to Mexico where he helps the wild Bethel Strange find her missing father. But there's an outlaw on their trail, and the next ones to go missing just might be them...

DEAD RIVER KILLER

Bad luck has driven Yakima Henry into the town of Dead River during a severe mountain winter—where Yakima must weather a killer who's hell-bent on making the town as dead as its name.

REVENGE AT HATCHET CREEK

Yakima Henry has been ambushed and badly injured. Luckily, Aubrey Coffin drags him to safety—but as he heals, lawless desperados circle closer to finish the job...

BULLET FOR A HALF-BREED

Yakima Henry won't tolerate incivility toward a lady, especially the former widow Beth Holgate. If her new husband won't stop giving her hell, Yakima may make her a widow all over again.

**Available wherever books are sold or at
penguin.com**

"A writer in the tradition of Louis L'Amour and Zane Grey!" —*Huntsville Times*

National Bestselling Author

RALPH COMPTON

S543

Also available from
Charles G. West

"THE WEST AS IT REALLY WAS."
—RALPH COMPTON

Way of the Gun
(Coming March 2013)

Even at seventeen years old, Carson Ryan knows enough about cow herding to realize the crew he's with is about the worst he's ever seen. They're taking the long way around to the Montana prairies, and they're seriously undermanned. They're also a bunch of murdering cattle rustlers—and now the law thinks he's one of them...

Also Available
Day of the Wolf
A Man Called Sunday
Death Is the Hunter
Outlaw Pass
Left Hand of the Law
Thunder Over Lolo Pass
Ride the High Range
War Cry

Available wherever books are sold or at
penguin.com